Western

Havill *B*

Leadfire.

LEADFIRE

By Steven Havill

THE WORST ENEMY
THE KILLER

LEADFIRE

STEVEN HAVILL

DOUBLEDAY & COMPANY, INC.

GARDEN CITY, NEW YORK

1985

All of the characters in this book
are fictitious, and any resemblance
to actual persons, living or dead,
is purely coincidental.

Library of Congress Cataloging in Publication Data
Havill, Steven.
    Leadfire.
    I. Title.
PS3558.A785L4   1985   813'.54

ISBN: 0-385-23018-4
Library of Congress Catalog Card Number 84-24670
Copyright © 1985 by Steven Havill
All Rights Reserved
Printed in the United States of America

First Edition

For Byron and Doris
and for Kathleen,
who makes it all worthwhile

LEADFIRE

I

I first met Doctor James McCuskar in the bottom of a deep arroyo, where he was being danced around in circles by a spooked horse. It wasn't funny at the time, although we laughed about it later—much later. What made it pointedly unfunny then, at least for the good doctor, were the bullets that sang by his ears and nicked at his black coat. And I, in my best cavalry fashion, came to his rescue.

I didn't just charge in. I had been riding for nearly twelve hours and was too tired and too surprised for that. I had been riding up Caffrey Cut, the deep, nearly canyonlike arroyo that led to the north, toward the little village of Coffee Creek. Caffrey Cut wound through the high, dry plains for many miles, and it afforded some protection from the dry blasts of wind that never seemed to exhaust themselves. When I first reached the cut, some hours before, I ducked my horse down into it, thankful for the opportunity to clear my eyes, ears, and mouth of the grit. I had ridden peacefully for nearly two hours when I heard the first shots up ahead. I stopped my horse and sat quietly in the saddle, listening. The shots were close by, no more than a quarter of a mile. Every time one of them peeled out, my horse twitched one of his sorrel ears and stamped a foot. I pulled my rifle from its saddle scabbard and levered a shell into the chamber before urging my horse forward, and I rode with the rifle butt resting on my thigh.

The arroyo took a sharp turn to the west, and just as I

rounded that bend I heard another shot, followed by a shout. After eight years in the cavalry, I still felt light in the gut, that rise of excitement, that tingling of nerves that makes palms go moist against the polished stocks of rifles. I gripped the heavy rifle a little tighter, with my thumb on the hammer.

Around another S bend there were two men and two horses. One man, blood staining his shirt a rich red, was trying his best to scramble up the steep sides of the arroyo while his horse—I assumed it was his—ambled down the cut toward me. The second man was still mounted. His horse was engaged in the damnedest dance I ever saw. The wounded man, making little progress against the loose sand and gravel, lunged upward on his hands and knees. After every futile effort, he would settle back exhausted, turn, and fire his handgun back over his shoulder. He must have been new at the game, because he should have just sat still, cradled that gun with both hands, and blown his pursuer out of the saddle. As it was, each wild shot sent the horse into renewed sun dances, and the big man in the saddle held out his own rifle for balance, like a tightrope walker.

The hammer clicked loudly against an empty cylinder. The wounded man dropped the revolver and pulled another from his waistband. He fired immediately. The shot must have been close enough to be noticed. The big man dove off the spooked horse and landed ungracefully with the muzzle of his rifle all but dug into the soft sand of the arroyo bottom.

At that moment, I saw the flash of a badge on the big man's vest. He regained balance and raised his rifle. I sat quietly on my horse and watched. I wondered if he was as poor a shot as the wounded man.

"Now stop right there," the lawman shouted, but he held his fire. The fugitive did stop, but not to give up. He turned once more from his efforts at escaping, and sat on the loose gravel, his mouth open. There was blood flowing down his chin. He was hit and hit hard, and he was game, but I didn't bet a plug on his chances. Less than thirty yards separated the two men, and from the shooting I had already witnessed, I was betting on the man with the rifle.

For a moment, gun faced gun. Then the Colt on the slope barked and jumped, and I saw the cloth of the lawman's sleeve jerk. The slug passed on and kicked up sand across the arroyo. Eyes wide, the lawman's horse ran past me, intent on putting distance between his tender ears and all the commotion.

Still the lawman held his fire, and I sat in amazement. He had nerves of steel, that was obvious—but I thought his brain was maybe a little soft.

Weakening fast, the man on the hill slumped a little, and the six-gun sagged. "Now give yourself up!" the lawman shouted. He held his rifle up. "You throw down that gun or I'm about to fire!" Sure enough, the fugitive started to raise the handgun once more, his face a combination of pain and determination. Even from where I sat, I could hear the lawman's rifle. He pulled the trigger, and the hammer went *snap!* Metal against metal. He worked the lever savagely, but the rifle was not about to cooperate. Seeing his last chance, the outlaw found enough strength to bring up his six-gun and level it at the lawman.

The man with the badge and useless rifle just stood there. I knew what was about to happen. His luck was set to run out. I brought my own rifle to my shoulder, aimed quickly, and squeezed the trigger. The heavy gun bellowed. The man on the hill let out a short scream and pinwheeled off to one side. He slid down a few feet on his belly and lay still. The lawman's rifle lowered slowly. He never looked my way, but walked carefully to the arroyo bank, his eyes on what was then a corpse. He made his way up the slope to the dead man, knelt down, and felt at the neck for a pulse. During those moments, I rode forward, keeping my rifle handy. I sat quietly, waiting until he came back down. He looked hard at me.

"I'm obliged," he said, and his voice was deep and so quiet I hardly heard him.

"And I hope you came by that badge legal," I said. He must have been nearly six feet four inches tall, and built to proportion. His dark eyes looked me over pretty carefully, took in the rifle, and then rested briefly on my army shirt, still reasonably fresh and clean. I'd saved it for the day I would reach town.

He stepped close to my horse and held up his hand. "Name's James McCuskar. I'm sheriff of Dalton County."

I shook hands, mine all but lost in his huge paw. "Who's he?"

"He," McCuskar said, turning to eye the corpse with distaste, "was one of three hoodlums who tried to rob our bank."

"Where are the other two?"

"The bank president killed them."

"I see," I said. "Well, Sheriff, that man there damned near killed you."

McCuskar nodded ruefully and held up his weapon. It was a small Winchester carbine, and looked to be either .38 or .44 caliber. He levered it open and held it so the sun shone into the action.

"Cartridge is stuck," he said, and jabbed at the shell with his finger. "Stuck real good, too." He slammed the action closed and sighed, then looked at me. "I didn't catch the name."

"Frank Buckley."

He pointed a huge finger at my shirt. "Army?"

"Used to be," I said. "I'm out now."

"Well, Mr. Buckley, I'm much obliged, as I said. But I'd ask one more favor of you."

"What's that?"

"My horse, and his," he jerked his head up at the corpse, "are somewhere down this arroyo. It's a long walk after them. I'll buy you dinner anyway, for what you did . . . that's the least I can do . . . but I'd appreciate it if you'd take a minute and round up those animals so I don't have to walk back to town with him over my shoulder." He grinned and showed very white teeth.

"I don't guess they went too far," I said, and I slid my rifle back into the saddle boot. It took no more than five minutes to round up the two mounts, and after that I watched as McCuskar lifted the corpse and draped it over the saddle. "Hell of a way to end up," I said.

"Indeed it is," the lawman replied. He tied the corpse down after covering it with a ground cloth. "Makes me sick when this sort of thing happens. No need for it. No need at all. Any one of those three could have done an honest day's work and been paid for it. Instead, they end up shot to pieces, for no cause. Makes me sick." He stood beside his horse for a second, looking at me. "I guess you saw all you need of this sort of thing in the Army. I know I did. Worst part of this job. The waste."

I wasn't used to hearing speeches like that from any lawman, and I didn't say anything. I waited while McCuskar gathered up the reins of his own horse.

"I guess all we can do is forget it and go on about our business," he said, and heaved himself up into the saddle. He settled down into the leather slowly, like a long, hard job was over. "Where you headed?"

"Coffee Creek."

"Ah. Then you can take me up on my offer for dinner. The

wife sets a fine table, young man. It's not much thanks for saving my life, but it's the best I can offer."

"I won't say no, Sheriff."

"Good." He spurred his horse into a jog trot, and I followed. We rode in silence for several minutes, and then he pulled to a stop and twisted in the saddle. "You know, I saw you when you rode up, out of the corner of my eye." A faint smile crossed his face. "I wondered what you were going to do, but the thought never entered my mind that you might be another partner to this one. Course, I didn't have the time to ask, either."

I laughed at that. "You were on the busy side, Sheriff."

"Yes," he said, and booted the horses into motion again.

I spent the next half hour watching his broad back ahead of me and wondering. James McCuskar was cut from a little different cloth than most sheriffs I'd met. How different he was, I had yet to discover.

We rode into Coffee Creek, and the place hadn't prettied up any. I remembered it from my youth, when I spent the first eighteen years of my life on the Circle B Ranch five miles from the village. Those were eighteen years spent in trying to find ways to get into trouble that would be entertaining but not fatal. There wasn't a privy in the village I hadn't tipped over at one time or another, more than once when the privy was occupied. There had been a fire or two with my name on it, and snakes let loose at dances. That, together with racing saddle horses for nickels and chasing jackrabbits, was about all there had been to do. On my eighteenth birthday, with mixed blessings from my widowed father, I rode to Fort Morgan and enlisted. I hadn't been home since.

The broken shack McCuskar and I passed on our way into town had been broken and vacant eight years before, when I rode out. There was less tarpaper clinging to the weathered boards now, and the roof was nearer collapse, but it was the same shack. The rusted tin cans that were strewn along the trail were probably the same cans, too.

The main street of Coffee Creek began with an imaginary line in the dust, and buildings cropped out of the prairie soil in two almost neat rows, one on either side of the ruts. A few homes, both shacks and well-tended houses, grew here and there to either side of the main street with its dozen or so shops, and I looked ahead and saw the big, pitched-roof frame building that had been only two years old when I left— the Sorenson Mercantile Company.

But like a half-thousand other prairie towns, Coffee Creek was neither wildly prosperous nor foundering. I guessed that maybe eight hundred folks lived there. To the south of the main street, down at the west end, grew a dark copse of cottonwoods that framed a large spring, a constant burble of fresh water that gave life to that thick oasis. The better houses were nestled in that circle of shade.

I knew where the one boardinghouse in town was, and I intended to steer my horse in that direction when a man on foot trotted out into the dust and hailed McCuskar.

"Hey, Doc! You got 'em!"

McCuskar didn't reply immediately, but he did rein his horse to a stop.

"Hey, Doc," the man continued, reaching up and laying a hand on the neck of McCuskar's horse. He looked back at the bundled corpse and then at me. He didn't recognize me. Ben Toby, small, quick, and wiry, was the town's jack-of-all-trades and probably the richest man in town. When I had left eight years before, he owned the livery—which wasn't much then —and he was also the undertaker, and any community makes both of them rich. Down the street I could see the double doors of the livery, with a horse or two standing in front. In bright lettering over the doors were the words HORSES BUY–SELL–TRADE. "Doc," Toby repeated, "Mary Patton's about to pop!" He wiped the hair from his eyes.

McCuskar looked tired. "She in labor yet?"

"She is that. Rice asks for you to come, soon as you get in."

"Well, I'm in," McCuskar said, and he handed the reins of the packhorse to Toby. "You might take care of this matter for me, and I'll go to the Pattons' directly." He twisted in his saddle and shrugged at me. "Duty calls, Mr. Buckley. Coffee Creek is about to increase its population by one, unless it's twins." He saw the look of mild confusion on my face and smiled. "I'm a physician," he said easily. I nodded as if nearly every day I heard of doctors who wore badges. "I guess I'm going to have to ask you to come for dinner at another time."

"I'm kind of dirty and smelly anyways," I said. "I'll just head on over to the boardinghouse. Give my regards to the new mother. If it's the same Rice Patton I know who's her husband, say howdy for me."

It was McCuskar's turn to look puzzled. Ben Toby was looking kind of sideways at me, and a slow grin spread across his face. "Well, I'll be go to hell," Toby said, stepping over and offering his hand. "Frank Buckley," he said. "You grown up some."

"You two know each other?" McCuskar asked.

"I guess we sure as hell do," Ben said. "You've been gone a spell, ain't you, Frank?"

"We'll talk later, then," McCuskar said. "I best get over to the Pattons'. Ben, if you'll take the horses, I'll be obliged." He dismounted, handed the reins to Toby, and looked at me. He was in a hurry to attend to business, but he was curious. "Thanks again, Mr. Buckley. Although it's beginning to look like maybe I should say, 'Welcome home.'" He nodded and walked off down the street toward the cottonwoods and the spring. I waved a hand at the departing Toby, then searched out a warm bath and a soft bed. It hadn't been much of a homecoming, but then I hadn't expected crowds of folks to be waiting by the side of the trail, waving flags. It was just as well. I needed time to blend in with the surroundings, time for other folks in other places to forget that Frank Buckley ever existed.

II

Sometimes, nothing fits like a hot bath. I had been riding the same hot, smelly horse for six days through hot, sometimes bleak country. Campfire smoke always blows toward the man taking his ease by the embers, and my skin had soaked up five nights of piñon and juniper smoke. I was fragrant. During those six days, I had passed by only one creek that was deep enough for a soak, but I hadn't taken advantage of it. And so, with all that, I had no difficulty in bypassing the saloon, such as it was, and getting right to the important things in life—water so soapy it could have lubricated wagon axles.

Ralph and Lulu Grey owned the boardinghouse and the saloon, both buildings dwarfed by the massive bulk of the mercantile that loomed up between them on the south side of the main street. For a dollar, I had dibs on Lulu Grey's shiny white porcelain tub, and there I lay and soaked for close to an hour, until I began to prune. Ralph was busy at the saloon, but Lulu wanted to talk. If I had let her, she would have been perched on the edge of the tub. They both had known my father—anyone who had lived around Coffee Creek until a few months before would have. She wanted to talk about the old man and about me . . . where I'd been, what I'd seen, why I was home. I fended off the questions as best I could and still be polite, and after a bit she saw how tired, and smelly, I was and left me to my recreation in the tub.

The room she gave me overlooked the street, and I pulled the curtains against the still-bright sun when I got back from the tub, clean and drowsy. I had given my laundry to Lulu on her demand, and she promised to have it ready, neat and folded outside my door, when I awoke in the morning.

That left me with a pair of pants and my boots, my gun belt and saddlebags. I folded the pants and put them on a chair by the bed, and laid the Colt .45 with its holster and wide leather belt on top. Then I turned and looked at the bed. It was narrow, with a fancy bedspread, and underneath were the whitest sheets I had ever seen. They put all thoughts of eating dinner out of my head.

"Damn," I said aloud, and fell face forward on the bed, asleep so fast I almost didn't have time to burrow my face into the feather pillow. Heaven couldn't have been any nicer.

The next day, the sun had a fair start before I awoke. I felt as if I'd been clubbed, but struggled out of bed, knowing I'd feel worse if I didn't. Lulu Grey had been true to her word. My clothes were in a neat, small bundle outside the door, and I dressed and went downstairs. She was up and bustling—for what, I don't know, since I was her only overnight customer that day. I sat down to a breakfast calculated to take more than ten minutes to bolt down if a man were in such a rush. I wasn't, and I enjoyed her expert cooking. After a bit, I did the only gallant thing.

"Why don't you find another coffee cup and join me?" I said, and Lulu beamed. When I had left Coffee Creek, only eighteen and not paying much attention to folks, even I knew Lulu Grey was one of the town's professional busybodies. I'd learned since then that having folks like her on your side didn't hurt. I watched her broad beam disappear into the kitchen, the bun of her gray hair bobbing with excitement. She returned, carrying a full and steaming cup in one hand and the pot in the other. She refilled my cup.

"It's been a spell," she said, plunking her ample figure down opposite me.

"Yes, it has," I said and smiled at her. Even gone to fat and age, she was still a handsome woman. Her eyes were bright with intelligence and interest. "And it's been a spell since I ate like this, too. My trail cooking leaves something to be desired." Lulu beamed and waved a hand, then changed the subject.

"We had such a nice service for your father," she said, looking faintly wistful. "He was such a nice man. Such a gentleman."

"I'm sorry I wasn't able to be here. I appreciate all you folks did."

"He didn't suffer, you know."

"I'm glad to hear that."

"Doctor McCuskar tended him. He's such a fine man. But there wasn't a thing he could do."

"I'm sure everyone did all they could." I sipped the coffee. "I met Doctor McCuskar yesterday, on the trail. He's new."

"Oh, mercy, he's been our doctor for almost three years, ever since Doctor O'Conner moved away." I remembered O'Conner. On the few occasions when I'd been forced to undergo any cure of his, I usually wound up hurting more than before.

"When did McCuskar hang on the badge?"

"That's been almost a year, now," Lulu said. "Last election. No one ran against him."

"Not even Ben Wilcox?" Wilcox had been sheriff last I'd heard.

"No," Lulu said, shaking her head. "Ben got tired. He never wanted the job, really. And James McCuskar is a fine man." She leaned forward and dropped her voice conspiratorially. "He has aspirations, you know. That's what I hear."

"Aspirations?"

"I hear that he wants the congressional seat in two years. The one that lawyer over in Coldwater holds." She said the word "lawyer" like it was somehow poisonous. "Doctor McCuskar wants to move his family to Washington. He wants his daughter to attend school there."

"That sounds fair enough."

"Well," Lulu said, a trace of disapproval in her voice, "he's such a fine man, the doctor is. I don't know how we will replace him. I really don't. Being sheriff gets him around the county more, you know. Most folks know the doctor, but this gives him some exposure, you see. I think he'll end up being a most important man, someday. But mercy, let me get you some fresh coffee and let's hear what you've been up to, young man." Before I could refuse, she had reached for the enameled pot. If I had much more, I was going to float. "Now," she said, "I never heard a soul say that you were coming home, Frank Buckley."

"I never told anyone." I smiled pleasantly.

She eyed me critically. "You've grown up. Age becomes you."

"I hope so."

"I remember when you left . . . what's it been? Nine years?"

"Eight, ma'am."

"Eight. Mercy, how time flies by. I remember when you left. Some folks weren't just too sorry to see you go."

"I, ah, cut something of a swath, as the saying goes."

Lulu laughed and clapped her pudgy hands with delight. "That you did, Frank. You know, your father used to show us some of the letters you wrote home. He said you'd been studying, even. He was so proud of how you'd changed."

I suppose the notion of me studying was strange to Lulu. I'd played hooky more than I'd gone to school, despite the whippings from my father. Learning was no hardship for me, but the confines of that little schoolhouse in Coffee Creek had been. It'd seemed more important to me then to learn how to catch a skunk without being squirted than to learn when Imperial Rome crumbled. You could do something with the former.

"Yes, I did some studying," I said. "Unless I wanted to be a trooper the rest of my life, I figured real quick that I had to know which end was up. I was kind of hoping, for a while, that I could wrangle an appointment to West Point."

"That would be wonderful," Lulu said.

"I guess it would."

"Your father said you made sergeant after just three years."

I wondered what else my father had proudly told these folks, but I just nodded.

"How long will you be visiting us?"

"I'm here."

"I mean, you have to go back. You have to rejoin the troop?"

"No. I'm out. I mustered out."

Lulu Grey frowned and looked disappointed. "Mercy, I didn't know that." She wouldn't have, of course. My father had died before even he knew. "We all thought you were going to make a career out of the army life."

"That's past."

"Well, then, my goodness, what do you plan to do?" Lulu

had no qualms at all about being nosy. If she'd been a man, she'd have been shot years before.

"I don't know just yet, Mrs. Grey. I really don't. I need time to get my bearings. Right now, I need to take care of the ranch."

That hit a soft spot. The son coming home to take over his old man's ranch after the death of the patriarch—that was a notion Lulu Grey could understand. A man would even leave the military to do that. The fact that the ranch hadn't seen more than a handful of Buckley cattle during the past five years didn't enter into the question for her. She nodded sympathetically.

"If there's anything you need, Frank, you just say so."

"I appreciate that."

"You'll be staying in town?"

"No. Much as I'll miss your hospitality, I'll go to the ranch," I said. "I thought I'd ride out there today."

"No one's been out there since your father died this spring."

"Then I'll be busy for a while with cleaning, I guess. The pack rats will have half the prairie inside by now." I stood up and stretched. I dug into my pocket and took out some coins, but Lulu wouldn't hear of it.

"We're so pleased to have you home, Frank. We're so pleased." I picked up my hat, and she rose and laid a hand on my arm. "Did you happen to hear about our robbery?" she asked brightly. "My word, three ruffians tried to rob our bank yesterday. Rice Patton, he's the president now, you know . . ."

"I didn't know."

"Yes, he's the bank president. Why, he shot two of them, right inside the bank. Doctor McCuskar rode after the third man and brought him in last night. Brought him in draped over the saddle. He went after him and brought him back, all by himself."

News traveled fast in a small town, but the events of the day before apparently hadn't been fleshed out for the folks.

"I heard something about that," I said. "I saw the doctor yesterday, when he came in." I smiled. "And I always thought Coffee Creek was a quiet town."

"Awful thing," Lulu said. But juicy to talk about, I thought. "Ralph was telling me about it." I agreed it was an awful thing and then excused myself. I was impatient, for it would be midday before I could be out at the ranch. I fetched my horse from the livery down the street, and exchanged a few words with Ben Toby. He was busy with the three corpses, trying to make them presentable before he planted them.

He came out of the small room when he saw me and closed the door behind him. "You look a sight more presentable than yesterday," he said and shook hands again. "Almost didn't recognize you. You've grown up some." He wiped his hands on his trousers. "Sorry about your father. He was a good man. You home for long?" I said I was. He opened the side door of the livery. "Boy!" he shouted. "Fetch Mr. Buckley's horse." He turned back. "The boy will have your mount ready directly."

I pulled two bits from my pocket and paid him.

"Jim McCuskar told me about you," Toby said.

"Oh?"

"You saved his bacon. That's what he said."

"I was glad to come along when I did." Toby ran a hand through his thinning hair, and a slight smile deepened the wrinkles on his leathery face.

"You still owe me a load of hay," he said, looking me over.

I laughed. "My backside still hurts, sometimes," I said. It had seemed as if my father had whipped me for half a year.

It'd seemed pretty funny when I dropped the hot coals down inside one of Ben Toby's hay wagons. It'd been a sight, watching those horses charging down the winter-white street, pulling the smoking bonfire behind them. The hay wagon had tipped over outside town, and the hay had smoldered for days. My butt had smarted for days, too. I heard hooves and looked through the doors to see my horse being led out into the sunlight.

"Nice horse, Mr. Buckley," the boy said. He held the reins tightly, with his hand right up under the horse's chin on the curb chain. Someone had taught him right.

"He's a good horse," I said, and gave the boy a nickel.

"I rubbed him down real good last night, and he had some oats this morning."

"Frank, we'll see you later," Toby said, and walked back inside. I mounted and smiled down at the towhead. He was maybe thirteen, freckled and eager to please.

"You'll spoil him," I said, and the boy beamed.

"Boy!" I heard Toby bellow from inside. The youngster waved a hand and scampered back to work. It sounded like Ben Toby was a little afraid I might be a bad influence on his helper. I rode out of Coffee Creek, out toward what was left of the Circle B. It wasn't much of a ride. Just outside the village, the prairie rumpled a little, and here and there a stand of scrubby trees dotted the grass. In less than five miles, I could see the small house on the brow of a low hill. Three big cottonwoods, more dead branches than living trees, sheltered the sod house. Behind the house was one roughly built barn, low and wide. I had helped my father build that barn when I was sixteen, after a fire of dubious origin destroyed the first one. That was all—a small barn and a smaller house. There were no fences any more, not even a corral. Someone had taken that down for firewood, probably.

I circled to the west, not riding directly toward the house. The place was quiet. The dogs were gone too, of course, and I wondered what had become of them. They were details, I knew, just details to become someone else's problems. Maybe they had gone to run wild. In the last two years of Thomas Buckley's life, before his scarred heart finally quit, there had been little at the ranch other than the two dogs, a goat, and a cow or two. He had written me about them, long letters that lamented his struggle with old age. The animals were his only company. He had let other ranchers run cattle on his land and had lived off the lease money. When his arthritis wasn't too bad, he had ridden into Coffee Creek to talk with old friends. He had died a lonely old man, and I felt a stab of regret that I hadn't been home when they laid him to rest.

I circled the house, holding a hundred yards out. No matter where a man rode, he couldn't remain hidden from the place. It sat on the knoll like a small carbuncle, dark and quiet. I rode directly in after making my circle and dismounted. I tied the reins to an iron ring that hung on the wall, not far from the front door, and then stood in the sun. I turned slowly to survey the place. The day was windless, and the cottonwoods were quiet. After a minute, I walked to the front door. There was no lock. My father had never believed in such things. If there had been no changes in eight years, there would be no bar on the inside of the door either. Just a simple thumb latch held the heavy slab door tight against the jamb, and I pressed it and pushed the door open.

The interior of the house was dark and musty, four months unoccupied except for a vagrant cowhand now and then. I left the door open and walked from one window to another in the front room. I swung open the hinged windows and unlatched the wooden outer shutters. The air, still as it was, slowly drifted into the small house. Things brightened up. I opened every window in the place—three in the front room and one each in the two back bedrooms. In the bright light that washed into the house, I could see that nothing much had changed in those years. In the front room, the big, old Royal cooking range stood black and heavy, with the dry sink beside it, and next to that the wooden barrel and hand pump. There was an old, musty Morris chair in the corner that had been old and musty before I left. A board rested on two empty nail kegs along the wall. Perhaps twenty dust-covered books of various sizes lined that makeshift shelf. The back rooms held little other than a couple hard beds. The hair mattresses smelled of mildew. Under one window was a rickety chest of drawers.

Knowing the kind of man my father had been, I knew exactly what had happened. At one time, less than a year before, he had written that he was "kind of cleaning out the old junk." And he had. He wouldn't have wanted strangers coming in to find him dead with all his personal effects around him, ready for snooping. He'd cleaned the place of all but the bare necessities. I figured that for the last few months he'd just sat and read, waiting. There wasn't a thing left, except for his books.

I leaned against the wall of one small back room and gazed out the small, high window. Beyond the knoll on which the house stood, the prairie stretched away to the horizon, a vast, unbroken green-brown ocean of short, overgrazed bunch grass. Far away to the north I could see the speck of another ranch. It was the better part of four miles away, and if the Browns still worked it, then Colin Brown would be looking for lunch with his wife just then. Brown was English. I had never liked him, but his son Stuart had been one of my best friends. Stuart had had a sister, a little, buck-toothed squirt who had always been in the way. I had no notion of what had become of her. Stuart had joined up at the same time I had, and he'd lasted for two years before he'd been bitten by a rattler. He'd been too far from the fort. He made it back, all right, but then he'd lingered in agony for nearly a week before he died. I missed him.

If I'd looked out each window of the old shack—where I'd been born and raised wasn't much more than that—the view would not have changed substantially. I rolled a cigarette, lighted it, and pushed myself away from the window. There were better places to live, but this was going to have to do. Its advantage was that I knew the place, knew every hummock and rill around the house, every crack and shadow inside it.

I walked back out of the bedroom and stopped dead in my tracks. James McCuskar was standing in the open front door. He about filled the opening, side to side, top to bottom. He didn't make a move to come in.

"Lulu Grey told me you might be out here," he said. He was wearing the same black, long coat as the day before, complete with vest and string tie. The heavy badge was pinned to the vest. The corner of the star was just visible under the lapel of his coat. If he was wearing a six-gun, it was stuck somewhere out of sight. He was certainly big enough, and his coat was full enough, to hide a cannon.

I stepped forward and beckoned. "Come on in. Dust off a chair and sit down." He glanced at one of the dust-laden chairs and decided against it.

"I wanted to thank you again for your help yesterday."

"First time I ever saw a man just stand and make himself a target," I said and smiled.

"Blame that damn horse for that," McCuskar said ruefully. "And once I fell off, there wasn't much of anywhere to go." He looked around the house with dark eyes that mentally inventoried everything they saw. "The reason I rode out was to mention to you that I'd need your signature on the deposition. I wrote up what happened, and I'll be sending a copy to Judge Baker over in Dalton. I doubt that with Rice Patton and a host of others as witnesses that he'll want a formal inquest. The whole affair was pretty cut and dried."

"I'll be happy to do that."

He nodded and reached into his coat, bringing out a wad of papers. He smoothed them out and walked to the small counter by the dry sink. "There's no table in here," he said, looking around again.

"Somebody helped themselves, I guess." He grunted and fished out a pencil. I stepped over and looked at the document and read it carefully. It was a fair account of the events of the day before.

"There's two copies there," he said, but I'd already figured that out for myself. I signed them both. I handed the papers back to McCuskar.

"Much obliged," he said and folded them back into his pocket.

"Who were the three men?"

"The robbers? Their names were in the deposition."

"I saw their names. Were they from around here?"

"I'm told their usual stamping grounds were east of here. Our bad luck that they decided to wander over this way."

"Theirs too," I said dryly.

"I suppose so. Yesterday I didn't place you. You're Thomas Buckley's son." He looked at me a little askance. "From what he said during the past year or so, you had quite a career going in the cavalry. I'm surprised to hear you've shucked it all." Something in my expression made him grin. "Course," he added quickly, "I don't mean to pry. Your life is your business." He hesitated just long enough to realize I wasn't going to comment on what he said. "The invitation to dinner still stands."

"That's not necessary, Sheriff."

"I know it's not," he said and straightened his vest. "But it still stands. I mentioned it to my wife, and she says tonight would be fine, if you'll come. About seven?"

"All right. Thank you."

"I live in Doctor O'Conner's old house, by the spring. You know where that is, I'm sure."

I nodded, and he moved toward the door. "You're planning to stay out here?" he asked.

"For the time being."

He looked around the small house again. "You're going to have to hire a maid," he said and grinned widely.

"I may think on that," I answered. I followed him outside and stood leaning against the side of the house as he mounted the big bay. My horse nickered softly.

"Tonight, then," he said.

I waved a hand, and he rode off, keeping the bay in a fast trot.

III

For the rest of the day I puttered around the old house, doing my version of cleaning and tidying. When I was satisfied I went back outside, where the sun was still high and hot, and tended my horse. Earlier, I had taken my bundle of clothes into the house, and now I unstrapped the scabbard that held my rifle. I took it and the heavy saddlebags inside.

I felt better, somehow, that I had let those saddlebags out of my sight for a few hours. They were safe enough—no one was likely to ride up unheard, and I was getting tired of guarding them. And then I remembered that the good doctor had done just that . . . he had ridden up as quiet as a ghost. I hadn't heard him until he was dismounted and standing in my doorway. I grinned at myself. I had tried to be so careful, and here a six-foot four-inch giant had padded right in on top of me. I shook my head and tossed the bags on the shelf, beside the books.

The rifle I carried over to the Morris chair, laying the scabbard on the floor. I settled back in the chair, enjoying the coolness of the little house, and tended to the gun. I was proud of it, big and heavy though it was. I had purchased it in Telsie Town—paid full price for it and been glad to do so. The wood was dark and nicely fitted, and the metal, still new and unmarked except for a little scabbard wear, was finished in a deep, rich blue. I levered the heavy action, and the Winchester flung out a big cartridge. I caught the shell as it hit my lap.

I knew many folks were favoring the .44-40 cartridge, since the same round fitted both six-gun and rifle. I thought that was convenient, but stupid. In a rifle, that cartridge lacked punch. I carried a Colt .45 revolver, and the rifle was a .45-90. If the two of those didn't do the job, nothing short of a military howitzer would.

I fished a bandanna out of my back pocket and cleaned the dust out of the big rifle's action, then polished the wood and the metal. That finished, I sat in the chair for some time, the rifle across my lap. I read the titles of the books across the room, ticking each one off in my mind. At bedtime, when I was little, my father had read me that one, but not the next. Whether read or not, they were all familiar. And then my eyes lingered on the saddlebags. If Lulu Grey had known about them, she would really have had something to gossip about. I got up, laid the Winchester down across the arms of the chair, and fetched the bags.

The old house wasn't designed for what I needed then. I had myself a problem. Thirty-five thousand dollars, even in mixed denomination, large bills, took up a good bundle of room—two saddlebags' worth, nice and fat and plump. I looked around the house and scratched my head.

"Hell, why not," I said finally and put the bags over my shoulder. I picked up the rifle and walked outside. My horse rumpled a long breath through his big, wet nostrils, and I stroked his neck before strapping on the rifle and scabbard, and finally the bags. I glanced once more at the small house, then rode toward town. Rice Patton had the best place for that money.

The Bank of Coffee Creek was the only brick building in town. Another was in progress, down a door or two from the saloon, and I figured that in a hundred years or so, Coffee

Creek would be solid, substantial red brick, one storefront jammed against the next, with all those fake fronts that rose above the rooflines looking silly from the back. Two elderly gentlemen were taking their ease on the edge of the bank's short boardwalk, and I tied my horse to the rail near them.

"Fella could get sunstroke on a day like this," I said pleasantly. They looked up at me, squinting. I remembered their faces, but not their names. "Maybe you gents would keep an eye on my horse." One of them—I remembered him vaguely as one of Colin Brown's men—allowed as to how he'd do just that. I walked into the bank, leaving my rifle and the thirty-five thousand dollars outside in the sun, protected by two nearly toothless old men.

Rice Patton had himself one teller, caged and secure. I looked around the bank and saw another woman, of indeterminant age, working off to one side at a small desk. Patton's own desk was on the opposite side of the bank, jammed in a corner.

"Well now, Frank," he said cordially, rising and extending a hand, waiting for me to cross over to him. As I did so, I wondered where he kept the shotgun he'd used to dispatch the two robbers. I shook hands with him and took off my hat.

"Sit down, sit down," Patton said. "I'm in your debt, I understand." He smiled.

"You had a busy day yesterday."

"Indeed we did." He brushed a stray hair out of his eyes. He was medium height and dark, still slender as a whip, and his intent face with its hawk nose gave him an aggressive air that his soft voice contradicted. "I hope it never happens again. You know, I woke last night—hell, it was almost dawn —and thought what a damn fool I'd been. I should have just let them have the money." He shook his head sadly. "But enough of that. It's over and done with. Say, we're pleased you're home again. My gosh, what's it been, ten years?"

"Eight. Seems like twenty."

Patton laughed. "Time goes by," he said affably, and he leaned back and hooked his fingers behind his head. He looked successful, and so did the sturdy little bank. "You decided you'd had enough of the army life, then?"

"Yes." I rolled a cigarette, and Patton watched me. I think he was still a little uneasy. Stuart Brown and I had had some good times at Rice Patton's expense before our trails led away from Coffee Creek. "And I hear your wife's expecting."

"We had a daughter, last night." He smiled proudly. "Just before midnight. I was afraid the unpleasantness yesterday might upset her, but everything turned out just fine."

Unpleasantness. I glanced at Patton. It wasn't every man who would gun down two armed robbers while a pregnant wife waited at home. Most men would have been just a touch more circumspect. "I'm glad to hear that. Is she your first child?"

"We have another daughter. She's three. I was hoping for a son, but . . ." he shrugged. "We don't get to choose our blessings." He leaned forward. "What are your plans? Are you figuring to take up at the ranch again? Was everything out there in one piece?"

"The place is fine. I don't know what I'm going to do just yet."

"It takes time. Anything I can do to help, you let me know." That was a polite way of asking what I wanted, and I got to the point.

"I'd like to leave a little money with you."

Patton nodded. "Fine."

"I sort of, ah, came into some money, and I hate to have it laying around the house."

"It will be safe with us," he said, pride evident.

"After yesterday, I don't worry much." I glanced at the teller and the other lady, neither of whom was paying us any attention. I leaned forward and picked up one of Patton's pencils, found a scrap of paper, and wrote the figure on it. "That much," I said.

Rice Patton raised an eyebrow slightly. Maybe such sums weren't unusual to him, but that much money would pay a dollar-a-day cowpuncher for ninety-five years. If it lasted me a third that long, I'd be happy. The banker cleared his throat quietly and looked amused. "I don't suppose you'd care to mention how you came by that?"

"It was legal," I said, and Patton digested that for a second or two, then nodded. He smiled faintly.

"Just so," he said and opened a drawer of his desk. He took out a long piece of paper. "Am I correct in assuming that you want this transaction kept more or less between you and I?"

"They'll know about it, won't they?" I looked over at the teller and the clerk.

"Yes," Patton said. "But they'll keep it confidential, I assure you. Either that, or they won't work for me. And I pay well."

"Then you fill out whatever papers you have to, and I'll fetch the money." I went outside. The two old geezers were still watching the street, the dust, and my horse. They nodded with understanding as I unlashed the saddlebags.

"Strike a little gold, sonny? Hey, hey, hey," one of them cackled.

"Just a grubstake," I said.

Back inside, Rice Patton grinned. "You're a trusting soul, Frank."

"Figured your reputation would keep the vultures away."

"That's one reputation I wish I didn't have," he said. In less than five minutes more, Rice Patton's bank had my thirty-five thousand, less twenty dollars I kept out. Before I left, Patton drew me to one side and quietly suggested that it might be wise if I were to make a will.

"If you die, heaven forbid, and if you don't have any relatives, the state will take all that," he said.

"You mean you won't get it? The bank, I mean."

"I wish we would. But no."

I told him I'd give it some thought, and as I left the bank I was feeling a little uneasy. Once a will's written, it's too easy to imagine it being read. And I had better cause to imagine that than most folks.

IV

The rest of that afternoon I spent wandering about Coffee Creek, refreshing old memories. I was surprised. Quite a few folks knew me right off, and quite a few of them came up to me to wish me the best of luck. I began to wonder if they knew something I didn't.

About six o'clock, after buying a round or two of warm beer in Ralph Grey's small, slightly shabby saloon, I went back to the boardinghouse and bathed again. Twice in as many days was something of a record for me . . . I had been a grubby little kid before I left for the military, and after that, fort life hadn't demanded much in the way of hygiene. My commanding officer had been about the worst slob in the army, and he hadn't expected much more from his troops.

Once bathed, I checked the crease in my hat, brushed off my clothes, and made sure my Durham pouch was full. I started to belt on my revolver, then hesitated. Wearing the gun wasn't exactly the sociable thing to do. When I left the boardinghouse, I asked Lulu if I could leave the gun with her. She agreed it would be gentlemanly of me. I went outside and removed the rifle and scabbard from my saddle and left those with her, too.

It was only a thousand yards to the cottonwood grove, but I rode anyway. I dismounted in front of the McCuskars' home just a couple minutes after seven and tied my horse to their fence. I felt a little uneasy. I had never met the doctor's wife, and Lulu Grey had mentioned something about a daughter who would make me sit up and take notice. As I went to the door, I was trying to remember how one was supposed to behave at a polite table.

James McCuskar was a good-looking man, with his giant stature, salt-and-pepper hair, and craggy face. His wife, Harriet, was as short as her husband was tall. She tended to be rotund, but was still stylish and prim. She tied her hair in a bun at the back of her head and had one of those fancy Mexican combs stuck in her silvery hair. She watched life through a pair of astonishingly blue eyes that fairly crackled with intelligence. And then there was Alice, just turned eighteen.

I saw her from the back first. Doctor McCuskar had led me into their parlor for a before-dinner smoke after introducing me to Harriet. The girl was working in the kitchen, and McCuskar saw me stare.

"That's my daughter, Alice," he said matter-of-factly. "She's busy with dinner, but if she gets a minute, she'll come in and be introduced." Just looking at that back, I would gladly have waded into the hot, fragrant kitchen for a quicker introduction, but I held rein. Her back was stunning. She had some of her father's height and none of her mother's fat. Streaming down her back was glossy dark hair that shimmered like a waterfall when she moved. I think I managed to keep my mouth shut, but I earned a brief, withering glance from Harriet McCuskar before she retreated to her kitchen domain after the initial introductions. Doctor McCuskar was a master of small talk, and I found myself nodding, half-listening. I occasionally found the opportunity to bend forward from the chair, as if I was interested in what he had to say. I was trying for a look into the kitchen. It didn't work well.

"What does Alice do?" I asked finally, not sure if my question fit into what the good doctor had been talking about.

"Do?"

"Yes. Lulu Grey said something about her teaching school."

"She does that. This will be her second year." McCuskar sighed and lighted a cigar. "We've never been able to attract a fully qualified schoolmaster here, as you may remember. After Mrs. Farley died—you learned under her, I think—there was something of a void." I nodded agreement, thinking irreverently that I would certainly have liked to have learned under what I could see of Alice. "Alice has had as much schooling as anyone," McCuskar continued. "She spent a year away from home, in Denver, at a girls' school. She's doing pretty well, I think. Kind of young, and some of the older boys give her something of a difficult time. But she's adjusting. I haven't had to shoot any of them yet. I'm hoping that in a year or two, if we go back east, she'll be able to attend either a college or a normal school. I'm not sure what she wants to do with her life, but schooling is not a bad thing, even for a girl. Maybe she'll be a nurse, heaven help her, or a full-fledged schoolmarm. Or maybe," and McCuskar grinned, "maybe she'll find some rich bachelor that meets her old man's approval and live the life of Reilly."

"You never know," I said. I refrained from trying for another peek into the kitchen. Philosophically, I reminded myself that maybe the older boys gave her grief because she had a face that would kill a healthy horse.

"That's right," McCuskar said, and then Harriet appeared. She wiped her hands on her apron. "I think we may be seated," she said. As we arose, and as McCuskar was about to say something, someone pounded on the front door.

"Now what do you suppose," the doctor said. He left me

standing in the parlor. I moved to the doorway of the short front hall, but didn't hear the conversation. McCuskar turned quickly, grabbed his hat, and stooped to pick up his medical bag. He strode past me to the dining room, where I heard him talking to Harriet.

"Mary Patton's hemorrhaging," he said quietly, and Harriet replied something I didn't catch. "Well, I'll be back as soon as I can." He kissed her on the forehead. As much as I wanted to meet the other half of Alice face to face, I didn't relish being left alone with the two women. I couldn't think of anything more uncomfortable, for them or for me. I stepped out into the hall.

"I think it would be a good idea if I came back another time," I said.

"Nonsense." McCuskar was brusque and didn't break stride. "Work up an appetite. Come along," he said, and I followed him out of the house.

"You want my horse?"

"No, it's just down the street," McCuskar said. I had to work some to keep up with him. We hurried out the short lane, then turned onto the main street. The Pattons' home was just a stone's throw from the bank, and was nearly new, freshly whitewashed and neat as a pin. McCuskar charged up the steps, pausing only long enough to say, "You stay out here."

It was a pleasant enough evening. I found myself a comfortable spot on the front porch and sat down. I pulled out my Durham and rolled a smoke. No doubt Rice Patton was inside. I wouldn't know what to say to him, so I sat quietly, enjoying the Durham. I gazed up the street and noticed that the saloon was noisier than usual, and then I wondered if the muffins would still be hot, or even offered, when the doctor and I returned to his house. Maybe his wife was used to such comings and goings. I didn't think I would have been able to live with it. I started to wonder a little more about the apparently lovely Alice, but the saloon drew my attention again. Things up that way were positively lively. Across the street, I saw Ben Toby's hired boy come out of the livery. He walked up the street with his hands thrust in the pockets of his overalls, head down. That boy worked a long day, I thought, and about then he looked up and saw me. He smiled and waved, and trudged over.

"Evenin', sir," he said.

I nodded. "And how are you?"

"Fine, sir." He looked tired. "I didn't see your horse at the livery. Will you be bringing him in later tonight?"

"No. I'm riding out to my place later on."

"I'll rub him down for you, if you want."

I shook my head and smiled. "He's fine. You'll spoil him. What's your name, son?"

"Andy Sorenson. Carl Sorenson is my pa." Carl owned the mercantile, and Andy had done some growing up since I had last seen him. We heard more noise from the saloon, and Andy glanced that way.

"I been in there a time or two," he said casually. At that astounding information, I nodded and then crushed out my smoke. I began to roll another one.

"I bet you have," I said.

He watched my fingers working. "You want me to light that for you?"

"I think I can manage, thanks just the same." He'd probably been practicing on his own supply of cornsilk—or maybe on some of his pa's tobacco—from time to time. "Aren't you late for supper?"

"Oh, it'll wait," Andy said. "My folks know I work late. My ma, she'll fix something."

At that moment, McCuskar came out of the Pattons', and Rice wasn't with him. The doctor closed the door behind himself.

"Evening, Doctor McCuskar," Andy Sorenson said, and the doctor nodded.

"Let's get to dinner," McCuskar said, and we left, after a reminder from Andy that he'd be happy to rub down my horse if I changed my mind.

"Nice enough kid," I said. "He sure works a man's hours."

McCuskar grunted. A window broke out of the saloon with a crash, but McCuskar didn't change course.

"Kind of rowdy up there tonight," I said.

"If Ralph Grey needs me, he'll send for me. He buys more glass for those front windows of his than any man I've ever known."

I shrugged. "As long as he doesn't complain, it's his affair, I guess."

"That's right. I learned that a long time ago. Folks around here work hard, and they need to play, too." We reached the McCuskars' front gate. "I don't always agree with their form of play, but as long as nobody gets hurt, what's the harm?" He looked at me quickly, as if to see if I had any arguments with that notion. I didn't and said so. "Besides," he said, holding the door for me, "most of them are voters. It pays for a man to remember that when he holds an elected office."

The drunks were about the furthest people from my mind by the time we were seated at a belated dinner. I was having a hard time keeping my mind on food after my first face-to-face introduction to Alice McCuskar, fine food though it was. McCuskar kept the talk inconsequential, mentioning Mary Patton's health, the weather, the events of the day. What I wanted to say was something like "Alice, you are the most lovely creature I have ever seen," but I didn't. Instead, I concentrated on not making a mess of my place setting. It was Harriet McCuskar who broached the subject of my killing the bank robber.

"My husband tells me he owes his life to you, Mr. Buckley."

"Well," I said, swallowing potatoes, "that may be a bit of an exaggeration."

"No exaggeration at all," McCuskar said quickly. "I did a stupid thing. You saved my bacon."

"He didn't have a posse," Alice commented. "He went after that man all by himself." She said it as if that were the bravest thing she had ever heard of, instead of the stupidest.

"I suppose in the Army one receives training to act as quickly as you did," Harriet continued, but I wasn't just sure who she meant. I glanced at her, but she was looking down at her plate. I let the comment ride and turned to the doctor.

"You were in the Army?" I asked.

McCuskar nodded. "Went right from medical college. Spent twenty years in the damned Army. Maybe that's where I picked up the habit of charging into things without thinking." He grinned and speared himself some more asparagus. "Where did you serve, Frank?"

"Little bit of everywhere. Spent some time in Oklahoma Territory, then the past years down in New Mexico Territory."

"That must have been exciting," Alice said. "Did you ever have to face the Indians? I mean, were you in any actions?"

"For goodness' sakes, Alice," Harriet said, frowning.

"Well, it must have been terribly exciting."

"Shooting people is not exciting," I said flatly, and Harriet looked as relieved as Alice did flustered.

"That's not what I meant," she said. "I just meant that the life must be exciting."

"It's dull, most of the time."

"I'll vouch for that," her father added. "She reads too much, Frank."

"Were you an officer?" Alice persisted.

"I left the cavalry as a sergeant. That's a long ways from being an officer."

"Well," Alice said, pushing her plate daintily away, "I certainly wouldn't come back to Coffee Creek if I had the chance to see the rest of the world. I can't wait until we go to Washington. That will be exciting. Father is going to run for Congress."

"I know. Lulu Grey told me that," I said. I could see right then that the McCuskars were going to have trouble keeping that young lady's mind on her book learning. She wasn't my idea of a schoolmarm, and I wondered what she had taught the youngsters of Coffee Creek when the one-roomer was in session. I was going to ask her about that, but the meal was finished, and McCuskar suggested a smoke and brandy.

We excused ourselves, leaving the women to clean up. McCuskar took a large cigar from the box in the parlor.

"Let's go outside," he said. It was cool under the cottonwoods, and the doctor worked on lighting the cigar. "You're going to work your father's ranch?" he asked finally, and I said I wasn't. He didn't look surprised. "You know, you may have come along at just the right time—other than being on hand yesterday, that is."

"Oh?"

"You've got some education, and you seem to have a steady head on your shoulders." He puffed on the cigar, and the smoke billowed up into the overhanging branches. He gazed out into the lane. "This isn't such a bad town, Frank. You grew up here. I won't ask you why you came back. That's none of my business." He puffed some more and turned to look at me. "Folks do those kinds of things. Town like this seems like not much of anything while you're here, especially if you're young and eager. Then, you put some miles between you and home, you mature a little, and after a time it doesn't seem all that bad anymore. You agree?"

"It's not any worse than anywhere else," I said. "Better than some."

"Just so." He tapped the ashes from his cigar and leaned against the trunk of one of the massive cottonwoods. "You know, there's more to this job than meets the eye. You may have noticed that yesterday." He grinned. "I thought I had the time for it. And maybe the inclination. Not sure now that I do. Something always comes up just when I don't have the time. Hell, we don't have enough crime to spit at, despite what it may have appeared yesterday when you rode in. And I will add again, thank God you *did* ride in when you did. But I never knew a county as small as this one, and as young as this one, could generate so much civil paperwork. It's absolutely amazing."

"You ought to have yourself a deputy or two," I said. "I'm surprised you don't." McCuskar grinned and clenched the cigar between his teeth.

"That's just what I was thinking, since yesterday. The job's yours, if you want it."

"That's not what I was leading to," I said. "I'm not looking for work just now."

"You will be. I don't guess a man like you can sit on his ass for more than a few days without having something constructive to do." He chuckled. "Sooner or later, your army pay is going to run out. Man has to eat. I'll pay thirty a month. It'll be worth it to me, believe me."

"I'm not sure that's the kind of work I'd be looking for . . . if I was looking. There's got to be plenty of young fellows around here who'd like the job."

"A few, maybe. Most of them work the ranches. I had two men ask me for the job, just recently. One couldn't read or write, so he's useless as tits on a boar hog. The other was a hothead who liked a fight more than anything else. That's not what I'm looking for, either." He pushed away from the tree and thrust his hands in his pockets. "You know, you didn't wear your gun tonight."

"I didn't think that would be appropriate, Doctor."

"You see?" His eyebrows shot up. "I don't want some two-bit gunslinger working for me. I want someone who uses his noggin." He tapped his head. "Now, I'll be the first to admit, you could have fired that rifle of yours just a bit sooner, but I suppose from where you sat, there was some thinking to do. I want someone for a deputy who the people of this county can trust. Most of these folks are good people. I don't want them . . . what's the phrase . . . rode roughshod? But I want someone who can act if he has to. You've proved to me you can do that."

"Anyone would have done what I did. And you don't know me from Adam."

McCuskar shrugged. "Maybe it's my habit of charging in. But no, most people wouldn't have done what you did, or they would have done it differently. And since you brought it up, answer me one thing."

"What's that?"

"Did you leave the Army with an honorable discharge?"

"I did."

He nodded and grinned at me. "You know, I had a chance to talk with Ben Toby for a while this afternoon. He has some interesting stories to tell about you—when you were younger."

"I bet he has."

"Some of them are true, then?"

"Most of them, probably. I'm lucky I didn't end up in jail."
McCuskar laughed. "The job's yours, if you want it."

"I'll think on it."

"Take your time. I could use the help. Maybe it's just that I
get saddle-sore too easy." We chatted for a few more minutes,
but with the sun down, the evening was beginning to chill. I
took my leave after telling the doctor it had been a pleasure
to meet his family. He grinned. "I'm sure," he said. "It was
our pleasure, believe me."

I picked up my rifle and revolver from Lulu Grey's and
then rode out across the prairie toward the ranch. Alice Mc-
Cuskar was on my mind most of the way.

V

James McCuskar had a flair for the dramatic. The next day I accepted his offer, expecting him to hand me a badge then and there. Not so. As I was beginning to learn, there was an electorate out there, and McCuskar took pains to play up the occasion. He sent a messenger to Dalton, twenty miles away, and two days later Judge Lucius Baker arrived in Coffee Creek. He drove in a small, black buggy with a canvas top, with a high-stepping Morgan mare pulling. It was a Sunday. McCuskar had asked me to go to church in the morning, so that folks "will see you're a God-fearing man." I was more nervous about facing all those duded-up folks than I was about facing God, but I did attend, and I did listen to the pastor, a fat, sweating man by the name of Randolf Feagin, lambaste everything in general and the lawless in particular.

That afternoon, there was a picnic behind the church, where there was some shade and a few strands of grass on which to sit. After the baked chicken and the lemonade and the potato salad and the pies, McCuskar gathered the folks into a semicircle, and Judge Baker swore me in. The judge was balding, short, and working on a paunch. When he pulled out the Bible and stepped up to administer the oath, I saw he had collected some potato salad on the edge of his mustache. He was more interested in getting back to the food than he was in dramatics, McCuskar or no.

"Do you swear to uphold the laws of this county, this state, and the United States, so help you God?" He said the oath like bullets coming out of a Gatling gun. I said I did.

"Jim, give this man a badge," the judge said to McCuskar. McCuskar pinned the heavy badge on my shirt and made a short speech. He told the assembled multitude—there were about fifty attending—that Dalton County and Coffee Creek were entering the modern age. He said a few other things I don't remember, because at that moment I was watching Alice McCuskar, who was standing off to one side with her mother. I caught her eye and winked at her, and she blushed. When the pinning was over, a few folks shook my hand, including Ben Toby.

"Frank, if someone hadda told me ten years ago that this day was comin', I woulda called 'em loco." He was smiling when he said it. Everyone went back to eating, and the sight of all that food made me queasy. I worked my way toward the edge of the eating masses. The way those folks were putting on the fat, it was probably going to be a long winter. I saw Judge Baker a moment before he pulled himself groaning into his buggy, stuffed to discomfort.

"Thanks for coming over," I said and offered a hand. The judge shook perfunctorily and gathered up the reins.

"Don't get yourself killed right off," he muttered and drove off. After a few more minutes, I excused myself, taking particular pains to smile my most engaging smile at Alice McCuskar. This time I got a smile in return, and a blush.

McCuskar had given me the key to the sheriff's office. That building was no more than fifteen feet on a side, all by itself, fifty yards behind and to the east of the church. It was strategically located so that when I stood in the single doorway, I could see nothing but the church, the back of Patton's bank and house, and the all-but-empty east end of the main street.

It was peaceful. Inside the sod building were a single table and two rickety chairs, along with a half-dozen boxes filled with various papers, some important, most not. On the wall near the door were a few wanted posters, all but two out of date.

The building had two rooms—the front room with the dusty furniture and jumbled files, together with one window too dirty to be of much use—and the cell. At least, I assumed it was intended to be a cell. It was eight feet by six, with no window and no furniture of any kind. A pile of old newspapers was stuffed in one corner. A heavy slab-wood door separated the cell from the front room. I looked in briefly and shook my head in disbelief. An industrious felon could dig his way out with a tin spoon in ten minutes, even through the thickest portion of the sod wall.

I spent an hour in the building, looking through papers and wondering why any man would willingly work in such a place. I quickly developed a system that would keep me sane and do the county some good. I talked Rice Patton into giving me a map of the general area. It was an old land-claim document, and I drew on the county boundaries as best as I could remember them. Before long, I began to admit to myself that it felt good, after eight years of regimented life, to be occupied again.

During the evenings, until I was sure the village was quiet, I spent my time in Coffee Creek. In the daylight hours, if no matters called for my attention in town, I rode the county, learning it all over again. I didn't need to bother much with Dalton. That village, slightly larger than Coffee Creek, had its own marshal. Old Clint White didn't have much to say to me. Maybe he felt threatened. He'd been village marshal for the better part of fifteen years, and a deputy United States marshal before that.

Once, when I needed Judge Baker's signature on a civil paper, I took time to offer White a beer.

"Ain't got time just now, sonny," he said, and stalked off. I shrugged and let it ride. I mentioned the incident to Baker, and he grunted something about White not thinking much of anyone younger than fifty. After that, I stayed out of White's way and let him run Dalton as he saw fit.

Things went smoothly for six days. By and large, I had ignored Grey's saloon, as the sheriff had suggested. On Saturday nights the cowpunchers liked to ride in, and they did a fair job of whooping it up. That particular Saturday night was cool, with thunderstorms brewing in the distance. I had been in Toby's livery, shooting the breeze with both him and his hard-working boy, Andy Sorenson. Andy didn't need to be working just then, but he was, industriously saddle-soaping bridles and reins and saddles until the leather glowed.

Ben and I were standing in front of the livery, watching the clouds build to the west. "Doesn't he ever play?" I asked Ben, nodding back at Andy.

"Ain't too many young'uns his age to play with," Toby said. "His daddy's a queer one, in some ways. Wants the boy to learn what work is about. When he ain't workin' here, he's helpin' in the store. When he ain't doin' that, he's doin' chores for whoever he can find."

"He'll never starve," I observed. As we talked, sounds other than the distant thunder caught our attention.

"They're havin' a time up there," Toby grinned. A window broke out of the saloon. "Quite a time."

"Rain's going to dampen spirits soon," I said, and I pushed away from the wall of the livery. "I guess I'll mosey on up that way. I'll be back after a bit. You might make sure the boy doesn't wear holes in my gear with all that rubbing."

I heard more glass break when I was a hundred yards from

the saloon. Glass breaking was a common enough occurrence, and I didn't see any cause to quicken my pace. I tipped my hat to a couple dour-faced old women and continued on. The noise from the saloon had tapered off, and I wasn't planning on entering Grey's domain. McCuskar was right. If they wanted the services of the law, they'd holler. A dozen steps from the swinging doors I was about to turn and cross the street, to make a pass around Patton's bank. Just then a cowboy staggered out of Grey's. Behind him were three others, equally shaky.

"You killed him, Harry," I heard one of them say, and then they saw me. Eyes went wide, first with drunken surprise, then with worry. If I had known what had happened inside, I would have been ready. As it was, I was off guard. The cowboy who had come out first saw me, then the star on my shirt. Without hesitation, he fought to pull his gun from its holster. Even drunk, he was skilled with that piece of iron.

"No!" one of the others shouted and reached out a hand to restrain his friend. I dove to one side just as the heavy revolver boomed, and my left hand went numb. I hit the dirt, drawing my own gun. By the time I turned, half lying in the street, the cowpuncher had taken to his heels, running toward his horse. His three friends stood stupefied. I lunged to my feet and sprinted after him. I grabbed him by the belt just as he hit the saddle. He still held the revolver, and he brought it down toward my head. I twisted, took the uncoordinated blow on my shoulder, and hauled him down. He hit the street on his back. His breath went out with a loud *whoosh*, and his revolver flew out of his hand. I dropped my own gun, grabbed him by the collar, and punched him full in the face. He brought his hands up, but there wasn't much fight left in him. He tried to twist out of my grip, and I punched him again. His nose spurted blood. When he was still, I reached down and grabbed my revolver. I thrust it back in my holster and pulled the man to his feet.

There was a considerable crowd of folks gathered to watch the entertainment.

"Did he shoot him?" I heard someone ask. They were staring at the cowboy with morbid fascination because the front of his shirt, under where my left fist was clenched at his throat, was turning bright red. I saw the blood and then realized it was pumping from my own thumb. The bullet from the cowboy's gun had clipped the end of it off, about halfway down the thumbnail. And about then it began to hurt.

I stared at it, releasing the man. He swayed unsteadily on his feet. "Why, you son of a bitch," I said. I punched him again, a coldly calculated swing that crunched his nose again, and I dumped him on the seat of his pants.

"Hey, now," one of the other cowboys protested and took a step forward. What little temper I had was gone. The pain in my thumb was making my entire left arm, all the way to the shoulder, pound in agony. As I saw him take a step forward, I jerked my Colt from its holster. The muzzle may have been choked with dirt from its drop in the street, but at that point I didn't care. I cocked the gun and held it straight out, inches from the man's face.

"Now you say one more word and I'm going to blow your goddamn head all over the street," I snarled. His eyes went wide, and we stood there for a minute, my thumb leaking into the dust at my feet. The four cowboys were so drunk they had no idea what to do.

"What's happening here, Frank?" I heard McCuskar say, and then his bulk was standing beside me.

"Sheriff, I think there's a man dead in here," Ralph Grey called from the door of the saloon, and a babble of voices rose from the street. McCuskar ran up the few steps and disappeared inside. While he was gone, the rest of us stood outside, waiting. Now and again, thunder boomed out, and the air was turning cold.

"I ain't going to do nothin'," the cowboy whose nose was threatened by my gun said.

"Bet your ass you're not," I said.

"He was cheatin'," muttered the cowboy on the ground. He still sat spread-eagled, and he spat blood into the dirt. The others were content to stand quiet, in no hurry to attract my attention. I waited, the gun growing heavy. After what seemed like an eternity, McCuskar came out of the saloon, face grim. Ben Toby had come up the street, and he was with the sheriff. McCuskar eyed the interested faces.

"Don't you folks have somewhere to go?" He didn't have to say it twice. The crowd melted away, some of them going back inside the saloon to view the apparent corpse.

"What happened in there?" I asked, and for the first time McCuskar noticed my thumb.

"You all right?"

"Yes. What happened?"

The sheriff pointed a finger briefly at the cowboy I had punched. "This one hit one of our local gamblers with a bottle. Hit him in the temple. Dead as a fish."

"He was cheatin'," the cowboy said again, plaintively.

"So Ralph says," McCuskar muttered. He stepped down and took my left arm. "Let me see that." He held up my hand and peered at my thumb. He glanced at my then-pale face, let go of my arm, and turned to the cowboy. Effortlessly, he hauled him to his feet. "So what did you shoot my deputy for?"

"I wasn't thinkin'," the man said. There were a couple snickers from the handful of folks who hadn't left yet, and

McCuskar glared at them. He turned back to the cow-puncher.

"You weren't thinking. You're damn lucky he didn't blow you right out of your saddle. He would have had just cause." He turned back to me. "Put that thing away," he said, and I holstered my gun. "You three, get out of my sight." He spat out the words like venom.

"What about Harry?" one of them asked, and McCuskar stepped up so close he almost stepped on the man's boots.

"Judge Baker will decide what about him," he snapped. "Now ride out of here before I arrest the lot of you." McCuskar sent me to his house, to wait for him there. He marched the quickly sobering cowpuncher to our "jail" and shot the bolt, leaving the man with the pile of old newspapers. I didn't share the good sheriff's optimism that the man would still be there when my thumb was tended to.

I stalked down the street, holding my hand and beginning to feel faint. I knocked on the McCuskars' front door, and Harriet answered. She saw the blood.

"He's on his way," I said, and pushed past her to McCuskar's examining room. I sat down. My ears were starting to buzz. I leaned forward, putting my head down, and hardly noticed Harriet as she spread an old towel on the floor under my clenched hands.

"Here," she said, and I looked up to see a good three fingers of amber liquid in a glass. I took it gratefully. "I hope you're not going to make a habit of this," she said, and there was a softness in her voice I hadn't heard before.

"No, ma'am," I said. I heard McCuskar come in some minutes later. If I thought my thumb hurt before, it was nothing compared to later. When the digit was repaired and bandaged, I was probably drunker than any of the cowpunchers.

VI

The thumb hurt, and I was irritated at myself for letting such a stupid thing happen. I also spent a few seconds wondering what kind of fool I was, to accept such a job when the bank bulged with my money. But I consoled myself that if I had to be alert and watchful, I might as well be paid for it.

Two days after the shooting, as McCuskar called it, I escorted the contrite cowboy to Dalton. He'd spent a quiet Sunday in the rathole that was Coffee Creek's jail. Maybe he'd been content to read the papers. He certainly had made no effort to dig out.

Judge Baker read the depositions, heard my brief testimony, and asked Harry McClung if he wanted a jury trial. The cowboy glanced at Judge Baker's sober face and said he didn't. Baker asked him if he planned on making a habit of shooting "my law officers." McClung again said he didn't, his voice a whisper. He looked at my bandaged thumb.

"What do you want to do, Deputy?" Baker asked me.

"That's up to you, your honor," I said. My thumb still throbbed, but it would heal. The gambler had been cheating, and McClung hadn't swung the bottle to kill. I probably would have fined the man and let him go.

"Five years at hard labor," Baker snapped, and the cowboy blanched. "And a hundred dollars' fine." He cracked the desk top with his polished gavel. "You'll serve time here until I decide where you'll go."

As we were leaving Baker's chambers, the judge nudged me in the ribs. "Didn't take you long to get into trouble, did it?" He chuckled. "When are you folks serving up some more chicken?" He went off, still chuckling to himself.

When I returned to Coffee Creek, wide-eyed Andy Sorenson was ready and willing, as usual. He took my horse, babbling all the while.

"Me and Mr. Toby ran up the street and seen it all," he said. He hauled off my saddle and staggered under the weight before placing it over the crosstree, blanket folded neatly on top. "How come you didn't shoot him?"

"You don't just shoot people, Andy. He didn't know what he was doing."

"You moved pretty fast, I heard."

"I like to stay alive."

"People thought you was going to shoot him."

"If I'd done that, I probably would have killed an innocent bystander. You can't hit much when you're rolling around in the dirt."

Andy inadvertently clattered my horse's bit against the animal's teeth as he slid it out. He wiped it clean with a cloth. He glanced at me and at the gun I was wearing. "You practice much, Mr. Buckley?"

"Give him some oats, too," I said. "And no, I don't practice much. Bullets cost money." The boy had put the idea in my head, though. After a quick stop to have my thumb looked at and rebandaged, I walked back up to the mercantile and purchased five boxes of .45 cartridges. I wasn't used to spending that kind of money, and it must have showed.

Carl Sorenson was a thickset Swede, and he laughed as he wrapped the five boxes for me.

"You planning on a vor?" he asked.

"No. But I guess I need some practice."

"Vel, dere you are, den," he said. I paid him, and he added, "The boy thinks a lot of you, you know."

"He's a good boy. Hard worker."

Sorenson leaned on the counter. "He loves the machines, machines of any kind. Dat's vhy he likes to vork for Toby. He'll be a blacksmith himself, someday. You vatch."

"He'll be a good one."

I walked back to the livery, and while Andy saddled and bridled my much-curried mount, I asked Toby if he'd have the boy take a load of hay out to the ranch when he had the time. I figured if I had the barn, I might as well use it. Winter would take some planning. While I was thinking on it, I ordered a load of coal as well. I even considered, with the thought of winter comfort in mind, returning to the mercantile to order myself some creature comforts—like furniture—but I put that off.

It was still early in the afternoon, so I rode out to my ranch and methodically began to practice what I had been ignoring for weeks. Behind the house, against an old juniper stump, I arranged a string of tin cans. I broke out the boxes of cartridges, and soon the air was filled with acrid smoke. In five minutes, I was thoroughly disgusted with myself.

A handgun, for me at least, was a limited weapon. With a barrel less than five inches long, my Colt was not intended for knocking elk off the top of a mountain peak a thousand yards distant, or even a hundred yards away. By the time I managed to hit five cans in succession, I had approached to within a dozen paces of my targets. For the next half hour, I bounced cans, trying for the bottom edge just for the satisfaction of seeing them jump and bound away. After a hundred rounds of that, I loosened up, firing from every position I could imagine, kneeling, squatting, standing side on, even sitting on my butt in the dirt. At the end of an hour, I was a little more satisfied, and my ears were ringing from the continuous barking of the revolver. I'd never make a trick-shot artist in a carnival, but I was better than average.

I slid out the twenty cartridges from my belt, and replaced them with fresh rounds. As I was preparing to fire off the last few slugs, I heard a wagon. It was Andy Sorenson, driving a team of palominos, and the freight wagon was groaning under a load of hay. He waved, and I walked out to meet him.

"Mr. Toby said you'd want the hay first," he called, "so I brung it out."

"Mr. Toby's right," I said. I climbed aboard while he drove around to the small barn, and then the two of us sweated while we forked the hay into the mow opposite the two stalls. My horse nickered and stamped and watched with interest.

While we worked, Andy asked, "Was that you shootin' a bit ago? I heard the shots while I was drivin' up."

I nodded, grunting as the handle of the fork nicked my sore thumb. "That was me."

"You pretty good with that gun?"

"Average, I guess."

"You must be. You was in the Army, Mr. Toby says."

I laughed. "That doesn't necessarily mean much, Andy."

"I go huntin' sometimes. Mr. Toby lets me borrow his rifle."

"That right?"

He grinned as he struggled with a laden fork. "I can't hit much, though. I don't think that rifle's much good."

"It's usually not the gun."

I don't think that registered with him, because he continued on, "I'm tryin' to get my pa to let me have a gun of my own. He's got a whole bunch at the store."

"I saw that he does."

"He won't ever let me hunt with 'em, though."

"They wouldn't be new if he did that."

"Well, he's got some that ain't new. I don't tell him that Mr. Toby lets me use his rifle." He looked at me quickly.

"I won't tell him either." Andy looked relieved, and we put the last of the hay in place. "That does it."

"Would you let me shoot yours sometime?"

"My rifle? I think it's a little big for you yet."

"I mean that," and he nodded at the six-gun I wore. "I'd sure like to learn me to shoot one of them."

"When your pa tells me it's all right with him, maybe," I said, and slapped the boy on the shoulder. We left the barn.

"He ain't never going to say that. Not for years and years and years and years. My ma neither." He shook his head and spat. Damned if he didn't have a plug of tobacco in his mouth. It was the first time I'd noticed. The boy must have had a stomach of cast iron, to be swallowing that stuff. He climbed up into the freight wagon and curled the reins expertly around his fingers. He was about to chuck the horses into motion when something crossed his mind, and the reins relaxed.

"You fixin' to go to the dance Friday night?"

I hadn't made one of the dances since I'd come to Coffee Creek. I had heard the fiddler sawing away, from a distance, but dancing had never been my strong point.

"I doubt it, Andy."

He grinned conspiratorily. "I hear Alice McCuskar's sweet on you."

"You hear that, do you?"

"Yup." He grinned wider. "You ought to take her to the dance."

"And why don't you get on out of here." I laughed and slapped the broad beam of the horse nearest me. Andy laughed and snapped the reins. "I'll be bringing your coal out tomorrow," he called, and I waved as the wagon left the yard. That clever little beggar was a matchmaker as well, I thought. Trouble was, now that the notion was in my head, it was hard to put it out.

Up to that point, my relationship with Alice McCuskar was one of wishful thinking on my part, unless, of course, there was some element of truth in Andy Sorenson's jesting. In many ways, Alice was still very much a child, but in other attractive ways, she was an adult—and that thought appealed to me.

Late that afternoon, I rode back to the village. As was my habit, I left my horse at the livery. Andy was off to a ranch east of town running errands, and Ben Toby opened the stall for me.

"Get your feed all right?" he asked.

"I did. The boy says he's going to bring the coal out tomorrow." I grinned. "I understand he likes to hunt."

Toby looked momentarily blank, then slightly embarrassed. "He goes out after them prairie dogs south of town every once in a while. I let him take that little Stevens I keep around for rats and such." He looked at me sheepishly. "I don't guess his old man would like it much, but hell, Frank, if I didn't let him do that once in a while, he'd might as well live down here." Toby shrugged. "I guess maybe I admire what Carl's tryin' to do for the boy, but the lad's got to play once in a while, too." I nodded and moved toward the door. Toby continued, "It ain't the shootin', either, I don't think. That boy likes just about anything with gears, wheels, levers. He's took that rifle apart a hundred times. He ain't going to be no squarehead blacksmith, like his old man hopes. He's going to be some kind of inventor, mark my words." He reached out a hand and tapped my elbow. "How's that thumb comin' along?"

I held up the bandaged hand and made a wry face. "Slow."

"And hey, speakin' of that," Toby said, "you hear that old man Taylor up and died this mornin'?"

"How'd he do that?" I stopped and looked at Toby, surprised. Malcolm Taylor was as much a fixture around Coffee Creek as the spring under the cottonwoods. He must have been in his seventies and had worked on almost all the ranches in Dalton County at one time or another. "I saw McCuskar this morning. He didn't say anything about him."

Toby shrugged. "Doc went out early this afternoon. Some folks passin' by saw something was wrong, went in, and found old Taylor, stretched out on his cot, dead as can be. They fetched Doc, and he fetched me." He turned and nodded at the door to his "office." "Body's in there, if you want to see."

"I don't guess so."

"Musta been his heart. He was an old cuss."

After a few minutes, I was back in the small building that passed for an office, and I found a note from McCuskar. The first sentence ordered me to his house anytime that evening so he could torture my thumb some more. The rest of the message concerned old man Taylor. The old codger had no relatives, and so I did what McCuskar requested. I rode out to Taylor's rude shack, just off the main trail east of town, perhaps a mile or so out. There was little of value in the place that the county needed to be concerned about, and I rode back to Coffee Creek about as lightly loaded as when I left. Whatever was left in that shack was just as well used by itinerants, drifters, or cowboys looking for shelter from the weather. It was a routine chore, and just as routinely I dismissed it from my mind.

About eight that evening, I walked to McCuskar's and did some more tooth grinding.

"It looks good," he muttered. I glanced at the discolored

member and silently disagreed with him. He cleaned it again and rebandaged it skillfully.

"You get out to Taylor's?"

"Yes. There wasn't much there. The old man didn't leave much."

McCuskar grunted. "I didn't think there would be. I didn't see much when I went out." He leaned back in the chair and wiped his hands. "Wonderful job, wonderful job," he said, grinning at my thumb. "That thumb will be a bit on the short side from now on, but otherwise, you're lucky . . . as usual." He stood up. "I heard some good comments from folks about the way you handled yourself. Everybody expected a shooting. Of course, when I got there, it looked like there still might be."

"I came close." I took a deep breath and frowned.

"Something else?"

"Well . . . I was thinking about the dance Friday."

"You were."

"Ah, yes."

"And?"

"I'd like to escort Alice." I finally said it and looked up at him, waiting. He grinned.

"So, ask her." Evidently some surprise showed on my face. "Frank, we're not jailers. Now it may look like that at times."

"Then you don't mind?"

McCuskar shook his head slowly, and he puffed his cheeks a little in thought. "I don't mind, and I'm sure Harriet doesn't mind, either." He pulled out his watch, glanced at it, snapped it shut, and put it back in his vest pocket. I had the feeling I was being dismissed, and so I stood up. "What bothers us, Frank, is that she'll fall head over heels for some local cowpuncher and be stuck in this one-horse town for the rest of her life. We have our hearts set on her attending school back east. We want her to see some of the world. After that," he paused, "well, then it's her decision. But we want her to have that chance."

"I was just thinking of the dance, Doctor. Nothing else," I lied effortlessly and smiled.

"Then ask, by all means. She's old enough to make up her own mind, whether Harriet or I think so or not. She's something of a romantic, as I've said before. She finds it greatly amusing that I was elected sheriff. And," McCuskar added, "she does mention you by name now and then."

Both Harriet and Alice were out of the house just then, visiting Mary Patton and the new baby. I didn't want to make a nuisance of myself by waiting until the women came home and resolved instead to ask Alice the first thing in the morning. I spent the rest of that evening, while I prowled about Coffee Creek, rehearsing my lines. The thought that she might refuse never entered into my conversations with myself.

VII

For the first few hours, it couldn't have been a better night. Someone had gone to an awful lot of trouble to fix things up, what with colored streamers and paper lanterns and all. The dance floor was prairie dirt, but no one minded, and the streamers were tacked to a board that in turn was tacked to the back side of the church, high up on the wall. The colored paper and cloth blossomed out across the dance area, tied nearly a hundred feet out to poles set in the sod.

There was a makeshift platform for the fiddler to stand on, and he fiddled and yelled out the calls with a fierce determination that far exceeded my powers of recall. Alice McCuskar was far better at that dancing business than I. Her folks were there, too, but they ignored us. When McCuskar wasn't dancing, he was most likely politicking. I saw him several times, huddled with other men, until his wife hauled him back to the dance floor.

I didn't wear my hardware. No one did. I had tethered my horse a few yards away from the merriment, just in case. Then I walked to the McCuskars' and escorted Alice up the street, her pretty dress all crinkles and lace and billowing.

When the time had actually come, and I had asked Alice, she'd agreed with an alacrity that did my heart good. I was proud of myself. I had made it sound far more appealing to stroll up to the dance, rather than riding in a bouncing buggy. We'd done just that, arm in arm, and more than a few folks had cast glances our way—envious glances, I'm sure.

She'd seen my horse and looked puzzled. She stepped over to stroke the animal's big muzzle. "He's a very quiet horse, isn't he?"

"Lazy horse," I said.

She frowned in mock anger and slapped the horse's big cheek lightly with the flat of her hand. "You let him talk to you like that?" He twitched an ear and waited patiently. Alice glanced briefly at my rifle in the boot, and at my revolver and holster hanging from the saddle horn. Folks had already begun to limber up with the first squawks of the fiddle, and she said, as she stepped away from the animal, "You're expecting trouble?"

"Hardly, miss. I just thought it'd be handy to have my horse here, in case I needed to make a fast getaway."

She smiled with delight. "Are you going to call me 'miss' all night, Frank?"

"Habits are hard to break."

"Does your horse have a name? I've never heard you call him anything but 'him.' "

I looked back at the gelding. "I've never thought about it. When I bought him, the fella said his name was Sammy. I didn't much like the sound of that, but never thought up anything better. He doesn't answer to anything except the sound of oats in a bucket, so it doesn't matter."

"Sammy. That's awful."

I agreed, and for the next hour we were too busy to exchange more than a word or two, brief conversations sandwiched between rounds of dancing. Eventually, even the fiddler wore out. We had finished the set with something interminable called a reel, with two long lines of dancing and clapping folks urging others back and forth between the lines. We were all flushed and out of breath. That's what the parson counted on, I'm sure. The lines in front of the lemonade jugs were long, and the donation baskets beside the jugs, tended by two sweet, elderly, and determined old ladies, filled about as fast as the jugs emptied. What the parson needed all that money for was a mystery to me, but after a couple summers of such, he'd be able to build himself a cathedral.

Alice and I got our lemonade. I saw James McCuskar and his wife chatting with another couple, and I stepped over.

"Frank, this is Hugh Mullen, of the Flying T."

"We've crossed trails a time or two," Mullen said, offering a hand. Indeed we had. The cowpuncher who'd shot off the end of my thumb, Harry McClung, had worked for Mullen.

The rancher looked at my thumb. "Sorry that had to happen, Deputy, but it could have been worse. I hope some time on the rockpile will sober old Harry up some. Maybe it'll do him some good."

I felt Alice's hand creep around and slip through my arm. At that point Mullen saw her and managed an almost graceful, short bow to her. She beamed in return.

"And the lovely lady," Mullen said. While Mullen and his wife kept Harriet and Alice company, McCuskar motioned me to one side.

"Everything all right?"

"Fine. We're having a fine time. I didn't know what I've been missing," I said. "I've got five left feet, but I'm learning."

"I see you are. What I wanted to say is this. I noticed when Harriet and I came over that there were still some folks over at the saloon." He smiled. "The nondancers, so to speak. I'd appreciate it if you'd take a turn around town, after a bit. I'll do the same right now. I'm not sure it's too smart, both of us being over here. Someone could walk off with the whole of Rice Patton's bank, and we'd never know. We'd look pretty silly."

I hated to admit it, but McCuskar had a point. I'd rather have faced a dozen bank robbers than leave Alice untended in that crowd of dancers, though. Out of the good dozen unattached young men at the dance, at least half of them were better dancers than I—and there was nothing like a graceful dancer to catch a girl's eye.

"Good idea," I said, trying to sound sincere. My face said otherwise, because the doctor grinned widely.

"I'll ask Ben Toby to keep Alice company while you're gone." His grin became even broader. "He old enough?"

"He's just right," I said.

I went back and rescued Alice from the old ladies. The fiddler was tuning again, and we joined a square. Out of the corner of my eye, I saw James McCuskar walking off, around the corner of the church. I sighed, and concentrated on enjoying the next hour or so, before I had to go to work.

During the break between dances, I told Alice.

"And here I thought everyone in Coffee Creek was here," she said. "My father is taking all this so very seriously, you know." And she patted me on the shoulder, shaking her head at the same time. Then she linked arms with me, standing close. The moment was too short, though. The fiddler was determined to do another of those reels. Lemonade profits were bound to soar.

When I left the dance, shortly before eleven, Ben Toby was a happy man. A little ridiculous, too. He was nearly a head shorter than Alice. I saw looks of speculation on some of the wallflower cowboys, and that put me in motion. From my horse I collected my gun belt, and then I took the county star out of my hip pocket and pinned it on, walking quickly toward the main street of town.

I went first to Grey's saloon, but McCuskar's fears were unfounded. No more than three or four men were there, quietly playing at cards.

"Evenin', Frank," Grey said, and he walked down the short bar. "What'll it be?"

"Nothing, thanks."

"How's the thumb?"

"Thumb's fine. Everything quiet?"

"As a church. But say, it ain't quiet over there, is it," and he laughed at his own joke. "Ain't you over there?"

"Was . . . will be again, shortly." I smiled at him and left. I walked quickly down the main street of town and reached the bank. The door was locked, the windows were locked. The place was dead. But up the street, I could hear the fiddler. I circled the bank quickly, then headed over in the direction of the livery. Ben's place was dark, too. Not even Andy Sorenson was working that night. I was wasting my time, and I turned and hurried back toward the music.

I was passing in front of the mercantile when I heard the noise. I don't even know what it was—just a small noise that shouldn't have been there, just loud enough to carry over the distant fiddle music. A cat, I thought, dismissing it from my mind. I tried the front door of the store: of course, it was locked. I stepped off the boardwalk and set off again, but another sound, the sound of squeaking hinges, stopped me cold. The noise came from behind the mercantile. I listened, rooted to the spot. Behind the store, there was only one set of hinges that I knew of. They were the hinges that held a single set of small shutters in place on the back wall of the store, high up off the ground. I listened and heard nothing else. Still cautious, I felt a sudden urge of duty. I walked as quietly as I could down the dark alley that ran the length of the store and rounded the corner.

Six feet off the ground was the opening of the window, and even in the faint light from a sliver moon, I could see the shadow of the open shutter, and I could see motion in the opening.

Instinctively, my right hand went to the butt of my revolver.

"Come on down out of there," I said, and took a step forward. That was as far as I got. A flash lighted up the small window, and there was a loud, but somehow muffled, gunshot. Simultaneously, I was hit a blow square in the center of chest that sent me staggering backward. I can't remember panic too many times in my life, but that was one of them.

"Christ," I gasped, going to my knees. The breath wouldn't come, and I knew I was a dead man. Rage took over from panic in those few seconds, and without breath and without hope, I managed to draw my own revolver. I don't know how many times I fired, because a buzzing was growing in my ears, and then I pitched forward on my face, the fiddle music in the distance fading away to nothing.

VIII

I became conscious of a cacophony of voices, and a heavy pressure on my chest. Then my head spun and the black void surged up again. That was the first time. The second time, I surfaced for a couple seconds and heard more confusing voices, more hushed this time. I wasn't thinking about dying. I was only thinking about the spinning and the blackness, and whether I could hold them at bay. I couldn't.

When I finally got ahold of consciousness for more than ten seconds, I was plainly surprised. I was in a darkened room, in a bed. It wasn't one of Ben Toby's slabs, and that was the surprise. Breathing was an agony. I moved a hand, inch by inch, and felt the thick pad of bandages. I heard a slight movement somewhere in the room, and knew someone was there. It didn't seem important. Sleeping seemed important, and I drifted off. That marching in and out of wakefulness continued, but eventually I became fully aware of myself, fully aware that I was hurt worse than I had ever been hurt before. I lay quiet then, staring upward toward the dark ceiling of the room. It was either night or the heavy curtains were drawn. I couldn't tell which. Each breath I took hurt with a profound ache that in itself was frightening, an ache that seemed to reach to the very core of my being, an ache that connected my breastbone with my spine in one long tunnel of dull, pounding hurt. I tried a deeper breath once, and gasped at the bands of steel that some monster blacksmith banged across my chest. I settled instead for the slightest, faintest inhalations I could manage.

Of course I was frightened. Dying was the last thing I wanted to do. But I knew of no instance when anyone had taken a cannonball through the middle of the chest and survived, even for seconds. And that's what I felt like. It was that thought that made me angry. I was still alive, and that meant I would stay alive. I didn't like debts, and I owed someone—whoever had been in that store window—a debt for making what life I had left a misery. That was on my mind when a shadowy figure bent over the bed.

"It's good to see you awake," Harriet McCuskar said. She bent down, her face close to mine. She laid a hand on my forehead. "You lie still now."

I had no intention of doing otherwise. I was curious and angry. My voice, when I found strength to croak a whisper, was distant and broken.

"Did I get that . . . that bastard?"

The effort of speaking made my ears buzz, and Harriet drew back from the bed a step. When she spoke, there was an edge. "He's dead," she said simply, and then I heard her leave the room. I went back to sleep, feeling a little better. I had planned on asking who the outlaw had been, but that could wait. He would wait.

The curtains were drawn back with a snap, and harsh sunlight filled the room with a brilliance that made me wince. I was feeling a little better, and less sorry for myself, and the sight of Alice McCuskar made it all the better. I admired her back as she adjusted the curtains, and she opened the window a crack so the air could drift into the warm room.

"Good morning," I whispered, and she turned quickly. She was not smiling. She walked over and stood by the bed, looking down at me for several minutes. Her face looked like it was carved from fine, white marble.

"My father said he'll be in after a bit. He said you should have some air."

"Thank you."

"He says you were very lucky."

I grinned weakly. "I'm sorry I didn't escort you home from the dance," I managed, and started to feel tired all over again. She remained a pace from the bed, looking down at me, still unsmiling.

"Why so glum?" I asked, and I saw a spark of something in her eyes, an emotion I couldn't identify. She continued looking down at me, and then some puzzlement drifted into her face.

"Mother told me what you said to her during the night."

It was my turn to be confused. "What did I say?"

"You asked . . . you asked if you had killed . . ." her voice trailed off.

I remembered the conversation then. "And she said I had." My voice was little more than a whisper, and Alice drew closer. "He shot first." I still couldn't read her expression. "I was going to ask your mother last night . . . who it was. I never found out who it was."

I have never seen a face dissolve into such total grief as Alice's did at that moment. Her eyes went wide, and she jammed her fist between her teeth. She spun on her heel and fled the room. I could hear her crying, and then I heard other voices, and I wondered what I'd said that could upset the girl so. If she was concerned for my welfare, it was a strange way of showing it. I didn't have long to wait.

The door opened again, and James McCuskar's bulk entered. He thrust his hands into his pockets and walked to the window. He looked out a long time, then turned, surveying me. His face was sober. "You're feeling better, I see."

"What's wrong with Alice?"

He walked over to the bed and bent down. A stethoscope was hanging from his neck. He looked at the wound, replaced the bandage, and listened with the instrument, brow furrowed. He must have moved that instrument to ten different spots before he straightened up, apparently satisfied. He stuffed the instrument in one of his coat pockets.

"What's wrong with your daughter?" I repeated.

"Tell me what happened, Frank." Maybe what his daughter thought wasn't important. I moved an arm up and rubbed my forehead. The arm felt like lead, and after the effort I let it drop on the bed. "Some son of a bitch shot me. I don't know who. I tried to shoot back. Your wife tells me I killed him. If I did, it was dumb luck."

"Perhaps."

"Perhaps? Either I did or I didn't. I was shooting by instinct. Who was it, for Christ's sake?"

McCuskar looked down at his hands, then back at me. "It was Andy Sorenson, Frank. It was the boy." The room went dead quiet. I stared at McCuskar and he nodded again, slowly. "Alice thought you knew," he said. He looked down at his hands again. "That was hard for her to accept, after what you told her mother. And after that . . ." he looked at me again, his face grave. "You really didn't know it was him?"

"Shit," I breathed, and turned my head so I was looking at the wall instead of the doctor's sad face.

"Frank . . ."

"Of course I didn't know it was him," I said, my voice a whisper. McCuskar stepped closer to the bed. "I didn't know it was him," I repeated, meeting his gaze once more. "If I'd known, I would never have pulled my gun." I closed my eyes. "I don't believe this."

"I hope to heaven what you say is true."

"What was he doing there? What was he doing, climbing out of the store like that? And what do you mean, you hope what I say is true? You think I'd shoot . . . God in heaven," I groaned, "What the hell was he doing there?"

"I was hoping you'd remember something, Frank. We've got to know what happened."

I shook my head and closed my eyes again. All I could see was the shadowy figure, squirming out of the window. "I don't know," I said. I kept my eyes closed, hoping McCuskar would leave. I felt sick inside, and I didn't want to talk anymore—at least not to him, not just then.

"Frank, there's a lot of folks out there who want answers."

"Now who the hell do you think wants answers more than me?" I shouted, and the effort cost me enough to make me even madder. I heaved myself up, supporting my weight on my right elbow. I hurt, but I didn't care. I glared at McCuskar. His face was pale. "Jesus Christ, Sheriff." I flopped back down, sweat on my forehead. "You tell me I killed a kid. It makes no sense he was there. It makes no sense that he would have shot me. Christ, it doesn't make any sense that I'm alive. Now you give me some answers, Sheriff. You give me some answers." I rested my arm over my eyes. "And no matter what anyone says, it's not going to bring Andy back, is it?"

"No, it's not."

"At least we agree on something." I turned back toward the wall.

"We're going to have to talk, Frank," McCuskar said. "Maybe tonight." He stood for a minute with his hand on the doorknob of the room. "I'll look in on you again. We'll talk about it. We need to. Right now you need rest."

I didn't respond. I heard him go out and heard the door close behind him. I spent most of that day staring at the wall, trying to lose myself in the patterns of the wallpaper. What had happened to me made about as much sense as those curlicues of color. There was no single fact I could latch on to, ready to say, "This is what happened."

Toward noon, Harriet came in with a bowl of broth that tasted awful. She didn't spend much time with me, and what little I saw of her face read noncommittal. Alice didn't come in at all. For supper there was more broth, and then James McCuskar returned. I had spent the day in thought, getting nowhere. I was finished feeling sorry for myself. The thought of Andy Sorenson dead was what hurt, but there was no bringing him back. As McCuskar came in, I said, "I want you to tell me exactly what happened, Sheriff. What you saw . . . what anyone saw." I returned his gaze steadily. "And I want to know when I can get out of here."

McCuskar looked at me for a long time, appraising, his hands thrust deep in his trouser pockets. Finally, he sighed and said, "All right, Frank. I'll tell you what I know." He drew up a chair and sat down on it backward, resting his big forearms on the straight back. "We heard some shots. No one seems to be able to agree on how many. I thought I heard four. A couple others say five. The shots came fast, like a string of Chinese firecrackers. A bunch of us ran down the street. Ralph Grey met us, and he told me he thought the shots came from behind the mercantile. We found you lying on the ground. Your gun was in your hand." He stopped and rubbed his face.

"Go on."

"Andy Sorenson was inside the mercantile. It was only by accident we found him. We thought someone had bushwacked you, then fled. It was only after we saw the open window that someone thought to check inside."

"And?"

"He was dead when we found him. Shot three times, Frank."

"Three times?"

"That's right." The sheriff picked at his fingers, his face grave. He didn't like going over the story any more than I liked hearing it.

"What about me?"

"What about you?"

"You've never said. What happened to me. I'm still alive, and I hurt. That's all I know."

"You're lucky, Frank." He got up and went to the cabinet on the wall, opened a glass door and took out a small paper envelope. He opened it and came back to the bedside. I reached out and took the lead slug from him. I rolled the bullet between my fingers. It was misshapen, mushroomed at the tip.

"Either .44 or .45," I said, and handed it back. McCuskar put it back in the envelope, and tucked that in his watch pocket. "You took that out of me?"

"I did. It hit you right here," and he tapped the center of his breastbone. "Hit you hard enough that it cracked the bone. It didn't go through, you can thank your lucky stars, but it tore a nasty hole, nonetheless. Lots of bruising, some bleeding inside."

"Then it hit something else first," I said.

"You think so?"

"I know so. At that range, any .44, or worse yet, .45, would have done more than that, straight from the gun."

McCuskar didn't reply to that. He was deep in thought, eyes focused off in the distance.

"What about Andy?" I asked.

McCuskar looked back at me. "He was hit three times."

"You said that."

The sheriff shot a look at me that was a mixture of sadness and impatience. "Frank," he said, "I've never found it hard to talk about things before. Things like this. I don't know." He looked down at his hands as if the answer was there. "At least one of the wounds was from a gun fired at point-blank range." He looked back at me as if he expected me to reply to that. I didn't. "Point-blank range, Frank. Hit him in the stomach." He pointed a finger at himself. "Came out his back. There were scorch marks on his shirt."

I was beginning to realize the depth of McCuskar's concern for me. "I was never that close, Sheriff," I said. When he didn't reply, I added, "What else?"

"One bullet nicked him in the upper arm, from the rear. The other hit him in the head . . . from the rear." Whether it was intentional or not, his emphasis fell on that word "rear," and his meaning, whether intentional or not, was clear.

"I don't care what it looks like, Sheriff. I did not gut shoot a thirteen-year-old boy and then finish him off from the back."

"I never said you did, Frank."

"Then you tell me what happened. Someone shot me. The bullet that hit me came from the mercantile. If that's the case, it could only have come from the window, where the boy was. I heard the shot, went down, and fired. I couldn't tell you how many times. But it was only after someone shot me."

"There was one round left in your gun."

"Then I fired five times."

"And at least some of those hit the boy."

"If you want to say three, go ahead, Sheriff. But that's not what happened. You explain who shot me, and maybe you'll have some answers."

"We're going to need some answers, Frank. There's already talk going around town."

"I don't give two cents for talk," I said. "And something else you never said . . . whose gun did Andy have?"

McCuskar turned silent again. His dark eyes bored down into mine. Finally he said, "We didn't find any other gun, Frank. There was no reason to believe he ever had one."

"Christ, Sheriff. I didn't chisel this hole in myself. I tell you I heard a shot. I saw the flash. As best I remember, the flash was up in the window. Maybe I'm not in any position to give advice, but it seems a good time to turn that mercantile upside down until you find something."

"We're going to do that. I've sent for Clint White. I think I'm going to need his help. I'd call for the U.S. marshal, but no one seems to have any notion of where he is."

I had never warmed to the old marshal in Dalton, and he certainly held no affection for me, but maybe McCuskar's idea wasn't a bad one. White was a cold fish, crotchety as hell. But he'd been around. He had more than his share of common sense. He didn't owe anybody in Coffee Creek as much as the time of day. If he was coming, it meant my skin was in his hands. It wasn't altogether a comforting thought, but it was all I had.

"I want out of here, Sheriff," I said. "I want to be on my feet when White gets here."

"You just keep your shirt on, Frank. We'll make sure there will be no complications."

"Complications about what?" I asked. "My health, or what happened out there?"

"Both," McCuskar replied. He stepped toward the door. "Would you tell Alice I'd like to talk to her?"

He stopped and turned. "I'll tell her that. But I think she needs some time, Frank. She doesn't know what to think. No one does. Give her some time."

"Then tell her that I wouldn't have pulled my gun if I'd known it was Andy Sorenson. Make sure she understands that."

For the first time since we'd talked, a ghost of a smile crossed McCuskar's features. "I already did that, Frank." He closed the door behind him. The room, still bright with sunshine, was completely quiet. I hadn't thought it possible to feel so completely alone.

IX

I watched the dawn through the lace curtains. The light spread across the sky slowly and the birds began their cheeping and cackling before the light touched the ground. I hadn't slept, and I felt miserable physically and miserable in the soul. But I was ready to be out of that bed, finding answers.

A little before six, I worked my legs to the side of the bed and swung them down to the floor. I sat up slowly and carefully. The bandage pulled, and I tugged at it tentatively, flinching at the result. I sat on the bed for some minutes. I supported myself with my hands flat on the mattress. Between my abused thumb and the hole in my middle, I was one big bandaged ache. I was about to try my legs when the door opened. There wasn't much need to feel modest. I managed a slight smile at Alice. "Egyptian mummy," I said.

"I beg your pardon?" She advanced and stood at the foot of the bed.

"I look like a mummy," I repeated. "You're up early."

"And you shouldn't be," she said curtly. "Father didn't say anything about you being up and about today."

"No, Father didn't. But if I spend any more time in this bed, I might as well be a mummy. I've got work to do." I rose shakily to my feet. Even in the early morning light, I could see Alice smile. I admit, I was a sight—half long johns, half bandage, hair unruly, and unshaven. Alice had good reason either to smile or run.

"I'm sorry about my behavior last night," she said, and held out a robe that belonged to her father.

"I am too," I replied. "And the less we talk about that, the better we'll both feel. And I'm not going to wear that. I want my clothes." I turned and looked around the room.

"Father didn't say anything about . . ."

"I don't care what Father said, Alice," and at that point, McCuskar walked into the room.

"Sit down, Frank," he said, and he jerked a beefy finger toward the bed. "Sit down before you fall on your face. Alice, the man's hardly dressed for female company. Why don't you go help your mother with breakfast. I think Frank is going to appreciate some solid food." Alice looked like she wanted to say something, but her father was obviously in no mood for banter. She nodded and quickly left the room. I sat down, like I had been told. "How do you feel?"

"I ache. A little dizzy. That's passing."

"Good." He went to the wall cabinet. "I want to change the dressings, thumb and all. Then we'll see how you feel about moving around." He set to work, humming to himself.

"When's White due in?"

"Probably around noon—maybe before." McCuskar glanced up at me. "I locked the mercantile and have the key. I didn't want anyone in that room until White had a chance for a look-see."

"Did you find the boy's gun?"

"No. I didn't look. I want to wait for White."

"I want to go over there this morning."

McCuskar shook his head. "Nobody's going in there until White gets here, Frank. There's enough talk going around already. I'll have no cause for any more."

"What kind of talk?"

"Just talk."

"I want to know, Sheriff. What are people saying?"

"Just forget it, Frank."

I pushed his hand away and he twisted his head up sharply and frowned. "I've got a right to know. It's my head." McCuskar grunted and went back to work.

"All right. I suppose you're right. They want to know why you shot a thirteen-year-old kid, Frank." He felt me tense, and said, "Hold still, damn it. You know how these things go. There's a different story every time you turn around. Every blame fool is an expert and knows just how it happened. I think the only one I haven't heard from is Carl Sorenson. He hasn't been out on the street since it happened. He was the one who let us into the store, and he was there when the boy was found. That was a shock, Frank. Harriet talked to his missus some, and they're taking it hard. They won't talk with anyone. They won't even go out of their home. But all the rest . . ." He shook his head in disgust, "All the rest blab their heads off without the faintest notion of what they're saying. All they're managing to do is twist what little really is known."

"And what is known?"

"What's known is that none of this makes any sense. You've got a hole in you that someone sure as hell put there with a bullet, probably spent, as you suggest. The boy is dead. That's what's known, and it's not too pretty a situation." He worked on in silence and finished his creation of another mummy. "And I'll tell you this, my friend," he said, standing up. "Now is not the time for you to be staggering around town, having to confront every so-and-so who steps in your path. Someone's sure to say something that'll make you lose your temper, and you'll end up in Ben Toby's. I'd hate to see that, after all the remarkable work I've done to keep you alive." He grinned, but there wasn't much humor in his eyes. "I have an investment in you, you know."

"Which story do you believe?" I asked.

"I think you know me better than that, Frank. I believe you fired your gun because someone shot you. More than that . . ." he shrugged and groped in his pocket. "You may enjoy this, by the way." He pulled out a newspaper clipping. It was from the sheet over in Dalton. I read it quickly and grimaced. The writer had done up his version of my confrontation with the cowboys, complete with "bullets criss-crossing the street like bees."

"Christ," I muttered.

"I particularly liked the name," he said and tapped the clipping.

"Bulkley." I shook my head and handed the clipping back.

"Keep it. Keep it. Make a souvenir out of it to show your grandchildren, Mr. Bulkley. I mean, to face down four desperadoes and only lose a thumb is commendable, don't you think?" He chuckled. "They got my name right, though."

"I hate to think what this reporter will do with the mess I'm in now." Another thought crept into my mind. Having my name in newspapers wasn't something I relished. Those little printed sheets had a way of turning an unknown place like Coffee Creek into smoke signals. That was the last thing I wanted just then. McCuskar didn't see the look on my face, evidently.

"Don't worry about it, Frank. There's nothing to be done, anyway." I didn't find that thought very comforting, either.

Marshal Clinton White arrived just about noon that day, and he had company. By the time White and Judge Lucius

Baker walked through the McCuskars' front door, I was taking my ease in the sheriff's parlor, sunning myself.

The judge entered the parlor and looked surprised. "For someone on his deathbed, you don't look so bad," he said. White followed him into the room, shot me a quick, dismissive glance, and went to reading the titles of the books on the wall shelves. The marshal looked like he'd slept in his clothes. Even his hair, white with age, was unkempt. It stood in little tufts when he took off his hat and ran his grubby fingers through the strands. Baker took a pace or two into the room and stood with his hands on his hips, surveying me. "You like getting yourself in trouble, son?" he snapped, and he looked down at the bandages. "I take back what I said. You don't look so good. You look like you stepped in front of a goddamned train." He jerked his head at White, who was still ignoring all of us. "Clint here has worked in Dalton the best part of twenty years, and without a scratch. You work for two weeks or less and stop enough lead to sink a ship."

"Just two slugs, Judge," I said. I held up my thumb. "And this one didn't stop much of anything."

"Let's not argue the fine points, Deputy," Baker said, and he walked to a chair and plunked himself down, hands on his knees. "Let's get this goddamned mess straightened out. I've got things to do."

"I'm sure Sheriff McCuskar filled you in," I said.

"He did," Baker said, "and I want to hear it from you. One of my deputies gets himself shot and in turn shoots a youngster, there's some explaining to be done. Clint here will nose around, and we'll have a formal inquest. Got to decide if there's to be a trial. I want your version first. First and quick."

McCuskar saw an expression he didn't like cross my face and said, "Just tell him what happened, Frank."

I did, and while I was reciting the short, grim story, I

wondered if White was listening to a word of it. Baker digested the facts and nodded. "Clint, what do you think?"

White turned slowly, glanced briefly at me, and said to the judge, "I think there better be a gun turn up, or Buckley's ass ain't worth a tinker's damn."

"Succinctly put," Baker said, and grinned at me. I didn't see what he had to be so happy about. He stood up quickly and grabbed McCuskar's forearm. "Jim, you and I are going to talk to a few folks. You said the stories were flying thick and fast, and I want them to know I'm in town and won't condone any rumors that interfere with what we're about. We're going to have answers, and then the law will take its course. You said you had a key to the mercantile. I want Clint to take that place apart until he knows just what happened." He nodded at White. "You do that, and meet us back here," he hauled out a big pocket watch and snapped it open, "at six. That gives you six hours. I don't want this thing lingering on. Jim, I want you to find a witness to go along with Clint. We don't want any talk about him fixing things. Who you recommend?"

McCuskar thought for a minute. "How about Rice Patton? He's the bank president."

"I know who he is, goddamn it. He's fine," Baker said, and the sheriff raised an eyebrow.

"I'd like to go with White," I said, and stood up. I felt a little shaky, but I was eager.

"You just stay put, young fellow," Baker snapped. "You so much as move a hair of your head from this house and by God I'll put some more lead in you myself."

"I think . . ."

"And I don't give a good goddamn what you think, Deputy. You'll do as I say." I stood a head taller than Baker, and I was glowering at him, but he met my gaze unflinchingly. The slight smirk on White's face didn't help my mood any. "Now listen, Frank," Baker continued, and his voice lost some of its edge. "I don't believe you realize just what a mess you could be in. You said yourself that you don't know hide nor hair what happened. Now, you let us sort things out. Any blind man could see you and old Clint here aren't the best of pals, but I trust him to find the truth, as best he can. I'm asking you to do the same. He's been around a good many years. He's saved my scalp on more than one occasion. Besides that, no offense, Clint, he's all we got. Unless you want this town to brew and fester till we get us a U.S. marshal down here from Denver. Weeks, maybe. You don't want that, nor do we. Now just trust us, damn it. Can you do that much?"

He stepped over and put a small hand on my shoulder. "Trust us some, will you? I think you're a good man, Frank. Just let us work to get you free of all this, all right?"

After a bit, I nodded. "All right."

"Good." Baker clapped his hands and pulled down his vest, tight across his belly. "Now, let's get to work. Jim, give the marshal the key to that sorry place. We'll get Patton over there as well." He continued firing out orders right and left as he and the other two men left the room. McCuskar was the last out, and he paused at the door.

"Stay put," he said unnecessarily.

I waved a hand and sat down. "I just hope that little fart knows what he's doing," I mumbled.

"If he doesn't, then we're all in trouble," McCuskar replied.

I don't know where Alice had been keeping herself, or how much she'd heard, but when the door slammed behind her father and the two others, she appeared.

"Hello," I said.

"You look tired."

"What bothers me most is not knowing what's going on out there," I said.

"Can I fix you some tea?"

I smiled wearily. "About six fingers of rye would do better just now. Where's your mother?"

"Over at the Sorensons'." At the mention of the name, she looked down quickly and turned toward the door. "Let me get you your drink." While she was out of the room, I slowly rolled a cigarette. A few minutes later, the drink she handed me was closer to two fingers than six, but it was welcome. I was still mighty sore, so I sipped carefully. A coughing fit was the last thing I wanted. I would probably have come apart at the seams.

"Thanks."

She nodded. "You probably shouldn't have it."

"Best thing."

"There's some baking I should be doing," she said, and made for the door again.

"Why don't you sit a minute. The bread or whatever it is can wait. I'd appreciate your company."

She did, an uncomfortable ten feet away, all prim and uneasy, and more beautiful than ever. The silence got uncomfortable, too. She didn't know what to say. I guess the notion of her father and me being the next best things to Wyatt Earp had lost some of its romance. I leaned forward and rested my forearms on my knees.

"I need to ride out to the ranch and get some of my clothes," I said.

Her reply was immediate and predictable. "You can't ride yet."

"If I take it easy, I can."

"Father said you were to rest."

I smiled. "Father said."

"Well, he did."

"Your father's a smart man, Alice. But he doesn't run my life."

"Don't be foolish," she said. "It's for your own good. And you heard what the judge said."

"Yes I did. You were listening, too?" She colored at that, and I smiled quickly.

"You're hardly well yet. It's been only two days."

"I realize that probably better than anyone else."

"Well then."

I took a sip of the whiskey. "I can see this is a painful subject for you, Alice, but I need to know when the boy's funeral is." She watched me stub out my cigarette, and when I looked up at her, she averted her eyes. Her fingers were twisted tightly together in her lap.

"It's tomorrow morning." She looked up and added quietly, "You're going to go?" I nodded. "I don't think you should."

"I want to, Alice. I liked Andy. I think I should be there. I'm perfectly capable of walking up the street to the church."

"That's not the point," she said, and her voice was distant.

"What is, then?"

"It's just that . . . it's just that the town's so unsettled. If something should happen . . ."

"Nothing is going to happen." I tried to sound cheerful. "The only thing that's going to happen is folks laughing at me dressed either in a robe or your father's duds." I stretched out an arm and pointed at the sleeve. "They hang on me like a miner's tent." She didn't smile, so I said, "I need to be there, Alice. I really do."

"Then I'll ride out and get your clothes."

"No."

Alice stood up quickly. "You are so stubborn! You are in no shape to ride ten miles . . . not even a hundred feet." Her face flushed with anger, and it made her look all the prettier. "There's a dozen people you could ask," she flared when she saw me smile. "Just don't be so foolish. Do what Father says."

"Father."

"Yes, Father! You be stupid and we'll have two funerals, instead of just one." She stamped out of the room. I had to admit, she was fun to watch, mad or sweet. I finished the drink and stood up. Maybe I was being foolish. Just then, I felt like the ride would do no harm. It wasn't as if I had a slug buried somewhere in my vitals. A cracked bone, a messy wound on top of it, some bruises inside and out—all it would really do was hurt some, and I could put up with the hurt. I left the parlor and walked back to the room that had been my cell for two days. My gun and holster, belt rolled neatly around them, were in the side cupboard. I had seen them when McCuskar had been rooting for bandages and cloth. I belted the gun on, noticing for the first time how heavy it was, and I had to tuck in McCuskar's shirt carefully so the baggy cloth wouldn't bunch down and catch on the hammer of the revolver. I ejected the spent shells from the revolver and cradled them in my hand. Perfect, obedient servants, I thought. They send bullets where they're told, whether right or wrong. I tried to dismiss that grim thought from my mind, took live rounds from the belt and thumbed them into the gun. On the way out the front door, I took my Stetson from the tree in the hallway. Outside, the sun felt good. I walked like a Sunday stroller down the lane, taking my time.

My horse was in the livery, and if I was lucky, Toby wouldn't be there. I hadn't seen him since the dance, and I didn't want to see him. I didn't want to talk about the incident with anyone. All I wanted was a simple ride in the sunshine. By the time I made it back, I'd probably sleep for two days—and maybe White, Baker, and McCuskar would have some answers.

The livery was empty. My horse looked up absently and I stroked his neck, then took the bridle down from the wall hook. I took my time, making sure the adjustment was right. It hurt a little, reaching up to buckle the ear strap, and after I did that I stood quietly, leaning on the horse's neck. "Why can't you saddle yourself?" I asked the horse, and I slapped him on the neck lightly. I put on the saddle blanket with no trouble, but the saddle itself was a different story. I pulled it off the wooden sawbuck and gasped as the weight pulled at torn muscles. I let it rest on the floor. From where I stood, my horse's back looked about a hundred hands tall.

I moved the saddle over in stages, and by the time I got all the way, ready to lift it in place, I was beginning to think that maybe Alice was right. Maybe I was a fool. I was about to heave the saddle up when a voice startled me.

"Now what the hell are you about?" It was Toby.

"I'd like to climb this saddle up on this horse," I said, and turned to face him.

"You look about strong enough to whip a day-old kitten," Toby muttered. "Here." He stepped forward quickly and took the saddle. Leather slapped blanket, and he bent down and grabbed the cinch, his fingers working deftly. After the last pass through the D-ring, he slapped the saddle. "There now. Where was it you was headed?" He stood with a hand on the cantle, and he didn't look pleased.

"Out to the ranch."

He shook his head and spat.

"I need some clothes."

"Somebody else could fetch 'em, you know."

"I need to get out. I need to stretch my legs."

"I suppose you do. I see Baker's in town. White, too."

"Yes."

"You know," he said, picking at a small scar in the saddle leather, "I ain't seen you since that night. I saw 'em roll you over. Thought you was a dead one, for sure. Glad to see you up." He shook his head again. "Damn shame it had to happen. I'll miss that boy. Probably more than anyone else in town, 'cept maybe his folks. I guess it sticks in your craw, too. Damn shame." He slapped the saddle again, idly, still not looking at me directly. "There's all kinds of talk goin' around, too." He paused.

"What are you getting at, Ben?"

He looked at me then and rubbed his mustache. "You just be careful, Frank. All this'll work itself out. You just don't do nothing foolish."

"Like what?"

He nodded at the horse like that explained it all. "Just don't do nothing you'd regret later. Here," and he took the reins. "Let me get him out of that stall for you."

He led the horse out, and I mounted slowly, settling down gently in the saddle.

"You ain't feelin' so hot yet, are you?"

"I'll be all right."

"Some asks, you want me to tell 'em where you went?"

"Like I said, I'm riding out to the ranch. But I don't guess that's anyone's business but mine. If McCuskar asks, you tell him I'll be back before dinner." Toby nodded and watched me ride off. When I passed by the bank, I glanced back. He was still standing at the door of the livery, watching me ride out like he didn't expect me to come back.

X

The two days I'd been away from my little shack seemed a lifetime, but nothing had changed. I sat down for a bit in the Morris chair, content just to watch the flies buzz around on the windowsills. The ride out from Coffee Creek had taken nearly two hours. There was no pace other than a slow walk that was comfortable. My horse hadn't minded a bit and very nearly had fallen asleep as he trudged. After resting, I pulled myself up and found some clothes. I packed them carefully in one of the saddlebags, then left the shack. There was nothing else I needed. I was about to mount up when I saw the dust rising in billows as someone came fast and furious up the lane from town. It was a single rider, and he was in a hurry. I could see his legs flying in and out, booting that horse for all he was worth. I stood by my horse and waited. The trail led nowhere but to my place. As he drew closer, I could see he was a stranger.

A small, foolish derby was pulled down on his head, and he wore a brown, nondescript coat. As near as I could tell, he was unarmed. His flapping coat revealed nothing other than a considerable paunch. He pulled the chuffing horse up abruptly a dozen yards away and walked the animal in.

"You must be the deputy," he said as he pulled his mount to a halt. The horse was sweating, lathered under his cinch and frothed at the mouth. I stood easy, my left hand resting on my horse's neck. My right thumb was hooked in my belt, with my fingers a comfortable distance from the butt of my Colt.

"I'm Frank Buckley. And you?"

The man was nervous. He glanced over his shoulder, back at the trail from town, then looked back at me. "Wayne Jensen. From over Dalton way." He made no move to shake hands, nor did I.

"From the looks of your horse, you've got business with me that can't wait. Something I can do for you, Mr. Jensen?"

"Well, I was kinda looking for some official information."

"Oh?"

His gaze shifted to my bandaged thumb. He was about to say something when his horse shifted abruptly, sidestepping a pace or two away from a deerfly. He jerked the reins savagely, pulling the bit up so hard the corners of the horse's mouth wrinkled back about to his hindmost molars. "Ho, now," the man said. The horse danced some more, then settled down, and the man relaxed the reins some.

"What information did you want?"

"Well, sir. I wanted to find out what happened with the boy."

"Mister, I don't know you from Adam. Just who might you be?"

He looked a little more nervous, and I could see his fingers tighten on the reins. "I, ah, work over in Dalton."

I took my left hand off my horse and faced the man straight on. I rested my right hand on the butt of my gun, and that move was not lost on Jensen. His knuckles grew white.

"And just what do you work at, Mr. Jensen?"

He coughed and turned to glance over his shoulder again.

"You seem a touch jumpy, mister. You expecting company?"

"No, ah, that is, I don't think so. No. I just wanted some

information, is all. About the shooting. I, ah, do some writing."

"Some writing. Would you be the fellow that wrote up that story about this?" I held up my bandaged thumb. He nodded and smiled a little sickly. He was frightened clear through, and I was beginning to understand why. "Bullets criss-crossing the street like bees? Or something like that?"

"You read it!" He nodded. "Yes, I write for the Dalton *Star*. In fact," he added, a touch of pride creeping into his voice, "I own it."

I stared at the fat little squirt incredulously.

"I just wanted to find out what really happened," he said again. I reached up with my right hand and rubbed my neck, taking a casual step toward his horse as I did so. Jensen's face was still trying to convince me he meant well when I reached out and took his horse's bridle by the curb chain.

"Mister Jensen, I appreciate you riding all this way and I appreciate a man who's got a job to do and gets right to it. And I tell you what. I appreciate what you've done so much that I'll give you about thirty seconds to ride out of my sight and off my land before I blow you out of that saddle."

"Now wait," he cried, and if he could have made that horse back up, he would have done so. "I'm not armed. You have no right . . ."

"Fine," I interrupted. "You're not armed. If you're not on your way, I'll pull you down off that saddle and beat the crap out of you, without the gun. How's that?" I smiled at him pleasantly.

"I just came for . . ."

"I know what you just came for. And I said to get out."

"The people have the right to know."

I was about to reply to that when I saw the dust. "That your friends you've been expecting?"

Jensen turned quickly in the saddle and followed my gaze. I could see what I thought were two riders, but as they drew ahead of their dust, it turned out to be one horseman in company with a buckboard. They were beating the trail for all they were worth. "Seems to be the day for folks in a hurry," I said. "Who are they?" As I said that, I jerked the reins clear of Jensen's hands. His eyes went wide, but he sat quiet, waiting, with his hands on the saddlehorn.

"I don't know," he said weakly, but his face said he knew full well.

"My day for company," I said, and held onto Jensen's horse as the others approached. If it was trouble on the way, there wasn't much of anywhere I could go. I had just enough strength to use Jensen as a shield if need be. Maybe he read my mind.

"I think I'd better be going," he said.

"You'd better sit right there." I began to relax when I recognized McCuskar's bulk in the buckboard. Clint White was riding point on his chunky pinto. Knowing who my visitors were, I let go of Jensen's tack and took a step or two forward. The newspaperman seized that opportunity to gather up the reins and jerk his horse off to one side. I glanced his way, and he was sitting bolt upright, expectant as could be—for what, I didn't know. For a man in a hurry to leave, he wasn't in much of a hurry. I frowned and turned my attention back to the approaching lawmen.

Clint White pulled up in a shower of dust, the buckboard close behind.

"Now where the hell did you think you were going?" White barked. His horse danced so that he was broadside to me, and White held the reins in his left hand.

"I've already been," I said easily. I nodded at the saddlebags on my horse. "I needed some clothes, and I thought I'd ride out here and fetch some."

White glared at me for a few seconds and then looked over at Jensen. "And what do you want, out here?"

Jensen was plucky, if nothing else. "It's a free country," he chirped. That collected him an icy stare from the Dalton marshal.

"Frank," McCuskar said, "come over here a minute."

I shrugged and walked over to the buckboard. McCuskar's voice sank to a near whisper. "Frank, you're a damn fool."

"Now wait a minute," I said. I was getting tired of being called that.

"No, you wait." He stabbed a forefinger at me. "I asked you to stay at the house. The judge ordered you to do so. The next thing we know, you're galavanting around the countryside." He lowered his voice another notch. "You know what Jensen wants?" I glanced across at the newspaperman, who probably wished he could hear the conversation. "He heard you rode out and figured to beat us here, in time to see a gun fight. That's my bet. He figured you were fixing to make a run for it."

I almost laughed. "That's on the stupid side, Sheriff. If I was going to run, I sure as hell wouldn't walk my horse out here and then stick around to be caught."

"I didn't say Jensen was smart, Frank. He wants to keep things stirred up. Makes for good reading. He tried to talk with Baker and White both, in town. Got told to go to hell. I wouldn't give him the time of day, either. His kind of news is not what we need just now, or ever, for that matter. All that aside, about the worst thing you could do now is ride a god-damn horse." He leaned closer. "How do you feel?"

"Tired of being asked that, Sheriff. I'm all right. Just tired. I was getting itchy, staying in the house."

McCuskar straightened up. "Well, no harm done, I suppose. We need to head back. Clint here has a few questions he needs to ask you."

"Let's get on with it, then," I said.

"I want you to ride back in the wagon," McCuskar said. "Tie your horse on the back." He turned to White. "Marshal, I want you to talk to that fellow right there and straighten him out." Jensen heard that and knew exactly what McCuskar meant. He puffed and postured, but White only nodded absently. I fetched my horse.

After we were moving, McCuskar turned and said, "If that newspaperman wasn't a good Republican, I'd be tempted to shoot him myself."

"I almost did it for you."

"What did you tell him?"

"Nothing."

"Good." We drove on in silence for a spell, and then McCuskar said, "I thought we'd find you by the trail somewhere, after Ben told me what you'd done."

"I didn't see the harm."

"Apparently not. Let's hope there wasn't any."

"Doctor McCuskar, you make it sound like I was on death's bed."

"That kind of injury, you never know. There could be all manner of internal bruising, even bleeding, that we don't know about. It takes time, Frank."

"Cheerful thought."

"Well, you just bear it in mind next time you decide to take flight somewhere. Judge Baker was about to issue an order to hang you on the spot when he heard you'd ridden out of town."

"What did you find out this afternoon? Did White find the gun?"

McCuskar looked sideways at me. "You have an irritating way of ignoring things, Frank."

"Oh?"

"You want the judge on your side . . . not against you. You might show a little concern for what he thinks."

"If he decides to hang me, I'll be concerned. I wanted some clothes. That's all. I wanted some fresh air. Now, you tell me what you found out . . . I've got something of a stake in this, you know."

McCuskar fumbled in his pocket and pulled out a cigar. He took his good time lighting it. "We found the gun."

"Where was it?"

"Slid under some boxes and other junk, maybe fifteen feet from the window wall."

"You're saying someone was inside and shot at me, then I shot the boy? That doesn't make any sense at all."

McCuskar glanced at me and puffed his cigar. "Not someone, Frank. Andy Sorenson."

I shook my head. "I don't believe he would have deliberately shot me. He would have never done that."

"He didn't mean to, if Clint White is correct in what he thinks."

"And what's that?"

"The gun he found was a Colt .44. It had been fired only once. There were five rounds still in it."

"One shot."

McCuskar nodded. "The slug I took out of you was a .44. That's what you guessed, and you were right. The ass end of the bullet wasn't damaged . . . any fool could measure it. What White thinks happened is that Andy had the gun in his hand and, like a fool kid, had it fully loaded. He wasn't familiar with it, or wasn't familiar enough. He was trying to squirm out that window, no way to tell how he was holding the gun.

White thinks that when Andy heard you, the boy panicked. Somehow, when he was twisting around, maybe trying to jump back in, or come the rest of the way out, the revolver went off. Hammer could have caught on the windowsill, the frame, even on his clothing. However it happened, the pistol went off. The bullet hit the boy in the gut, passed clean through, and then hit you."

"If I hadn't fired, then . . ."

McCuskar shook his head quickly. "It wouldn't have mattered, Frank. That first slug was fired at point-blank range. The way he was all scrunched up, it did a lot of damage. The boy was already as good as dead when you shot—and you shot out of reflex, nothing else."

I looked down at my hands. "Whose gun was it?"

"Carl Sorenson came out of his house today. I had a chance to talk with him. He recognized the gun. He said it belonged to old man Taylor."

"Taylor? Malcolm Taylor? That old coot who died a bit ago, out east of town?"

"The same. The way I figure it is that Andy must have passed by there sometime during the day, after I was out there, but before you showed up to clean out the place. That's all we can come up with. Carl says Andy made a delivery out that way, that afternoon, for Ben Toby. Maybe he had heard all the stories about old Taylor having no kin and couldn't resist poking around in that shack. He saw the gun and figured there was no harm in taking it. Be just like a kid to spirit something like that away. He probably thought no one would ever know."

"Then what was he doing in the store?"

"Ammunition, we guess. Carl says he keeps loose rounds of ammunition in an old cigar box under the counter. Be like old Taylor not to have any, except maybe the few rounds that were in the gun, if even that. My guess is that Andy knew his father would never miss a few loose rounds. Probably planned to slip out someday and shoot at prairie dogs."

"What's Sorenson saying? I mean, how's he taking it?"

McCuskar sighed. "He's coming to terms with what happened, Frank. I don't think he blames you. At least he never said he did. I tried to explain what we think happened. I tried to be gentle with him, but honest at the same time. Carl's blaming himself, more than anything else."

"What happens now, then?"

"Judge Baker wants a formal inquest, Frank. A public one. He's a stickler for following the letter of the law. He wants all the information, and then an inquest, so he can make up his mind whether there should be a trial."

"Trial? I thought you just said it was all an accident. There's a need for a trial?"

"I said we figured what happened. I'm not saying we know for sure, or ever will. It's all guesswork, Frank. The only thing we're sure of is that there was no one else, other than the boy. No one could have crawled out that window afterward without leaving a trace. There was enough blood on that sill that marks would have shown clear as day. No one went out the front door. There's no reason to believe the boy was other than alone. If that's true, then what I've described is the only way we could imagine it happening. There's a couple things Clint wants to ask you, and after that, it's up to Baker to decide."

"What's the marshal want?"

"I don't know. He wouldn't say. Just some loose ends, I guess." He looked over at me and twitched the cigar to the other side of his mouth. "That's when we found out you had ridden out of town. We came to talk to you, and Alice told us. Toby, too. That's when the reporter heard about it, over at the livery. He lit out ahead of us." McCuskar twisted in his seat and looked to the rear. White was riding perhaps a hundred feet behind us, and there was no sign of Jensen. "Looks like White convinced our newspaperman," McCuskar said. "We don't need him, not now. Just the wrong time for vultures like him."

The sheriff frowned and pulled on the cigar. "Folks are still tossing rumors, Frank," he said. "That's why we've got to be so careful. Enough folks saw you stick that gun in the cowboy's face last week, and I know some figure you to be a hothead. It makes better talk deciding you're guilty of something other than acting out of instinct. You have ten men, you have ten experts. You know how it is. And not one of them knows a goddamned thing. The Sorenson boy was well thought of. His death goes hard, any way you look at it. But I guess I don't have to tell you that."

"No, you don't."

I watched the tall grass pass under the horse's hooves and thought about how I'd like to have been able to turn the clock back.

"By the way," McCuskar said, "Alice told me you want to go to the funeral tomorrow."

"I do."

"I'm not sure that's a good idea."

"Good idea or not, I'm going."

"We'll see," he said, "We'll see."

"There's no seeing about it. I'm going. I owe it to the boy's folks."

"Frank," McCuskar said wearily, "think a little before you plunge into things, will you? Let's proceed with a bit of care. Maybe now, the less folks see of you, the better for all of us. Until this blows over."

"Yeah, there are voters out there, Sheriff," I said dryly, and McCuskar turned quickly, frowning.

"That's not what I meant."

"No, but it's on your mind."

The buckboard stopped with a jolt as McCuskar hauled back on the reins. He shifted in his seat, and I could see the anger on his face. "Now listen to me, young fellow. You don't tell me what's on my mind. You may not have noticed, but there's a passel of folks in town who would like nothing better than a little entertainment at your expense. You don't know these people like I do and coupled with that is that marvelous capacity of yours not to notice what's going on under your nose, unless someone is shooting at you. I say that if you walk into a crowd gathered at the church, you're asking for it. You're asking to start something that doesn't need to be started. Someone's going to say something, and you, like a damned fool, aren't going to be able to keep your trap shut. And there we'll be." He chucked the reins and the horse stepped out again. "Just leave it be for a while, Frank. I can understand you wanting to be there. But let it be."

We rode the rest of the way into Coffee Creek in silence. When we hit town, Clint White was riding beside the buckboard. I half-expected to see Judge Lucius Baker standing in the middle of the street holding a hangman's noose. He wasn't.

XI

I think James McCuskar was wrong. Clint White and I walked over to the mercantile after I rested for an hour or so. Both White and I were impatient, but McCuskar was adamant. When we did make the trip, the only reaction I got was a couple nods from folks on the street. Maybe McCuskar, in his roaming about town, had seen or heard things that I hadn't. But the people seemed the same sensible, hardworking folks that they had been ever since my homecoming weeks before.

White still wasn't much for words, and what he wanted was simple enough. I showed him where I remembered standing, as best I could. He asked me to go to my knees, and point my gun at the window. That brought back the memories with a painful intensity, but I did as he asked. He stood off to one side, hand on his chin, thinking. I could see his eyes drawing lines in the air between me and that window. Finally, satisfied, he grunted and we left the alley.

"When's the judge want the inquest?" I asked as we walked back to the street.

"Don't know, sonny," White said. I didn't give him the satisfaction of pursuing the conversation. We walked back to the lane by the cottonwoods in silence. When we reached McCuskar's gate, he turned.

"I'll be at the boardin' house if the sheriff needs me," he said, and stalked off, taciturn as ever.

I had been escorted, and that irked me. "It was kind of you to walk me home," I called after him, but he ignored me. When I went inside, I was not in the best of moods. Harriet met me in the hallway.

"James is with a patient, but he won't be long. Would you like something to keep you until dinner, or can you wait? We'll be eating about seven."

"I'm fine, ma'am. I'll just light in the parlor if I may. I'll be staying at Grey's tonight. I think I've been in your hair long enough."

She smiled. "Nonsense. And I don't think my husband would have it, anyway. He wants to keep an eye on you for another day or two. He's still worried about you."

Indeed he is, I thought. *He wants to keep an eye on me as sheriff, but not as physician.* "I'm fine, ma'am," I said.

"Well, you talk to him first. You're welcome here. We have the room, heaven knows. Are you sure I can't get you something?"

"No ma'am. Thank you."

I settled into the softest chair the parlor had to offer and rolled myself a cigarette. It takes a while to do that with only one good thumb, but I managed, spilling a minimum of tobacco in my lap.

"You're very good at that." Alice could pad about as silently as her father, and I started. She smiled and handed me a small glass of amber medicine. "Mother felt you should have this."

"Your mother's a smart woman, Alice." I took it from her. "I made it there and back, as you can see."

"Pride cometh before a fall," she said, but she said it with a smile.

"Goodness."

"Well, it does. You should be careful."

"Are you always so careful?"

"What do you mean by that?" she frowned.

"I mean, do you always sit clear on the other side of the room from your company?"

She laughed, blushed, and flounced over to the chair that was near mine, the two of us separated only by the small table. "How's that?" She sat with her hands folded in her lap, prim as you please.

"That's better. When's the next dance?"

A cloud shadowed her face, and she looked down. "I don't think people are ready for another dance, not just yet." I watched her face for a while.

"I said the wrong thing, didn't I?"

"No," she sighed. "No. This has been a terrible time. I think it has."

"Things like this happen once in a while."

"To you?"

"No. Not to me. Never anything like this."

"I hope never again," she said, and looked up at me. "I don't see how you can be so calm. Was it the Army that did that to you?"

"Did what?"

"You seem so . . . so detached from it all. Was it the Army that taught you to blank things out of your mind?"

"I didn't realize that's what I did. There isn't much I can do about anything, not just now."

"I suppose not."

"What would you have me do?" She didn't have the opportunity to answer, if an answer she had, because her father came into the parlor. He nodded curtly at the two of us.

"You're a busy man, Doctor," I said.

"Boy with an impacted tooth," McCuskar grunted. "Messy things. Alice, I need to talk to Frank. Excuse us, please. Tell your mother we're not to be disturbed." The girl glanced at me and got to her feet. "Maybe you'd bring me one of those first," her father added, indicating the drink I was nursing. "You want another one?" I shook my head. Alice went out. I was curious about McCuskar's brusque manner. "White back at the boardinghouse?" he asked.

"Knocking heads with Judge Baker, I expect," I answered. "White had me explain what I remember . . . for the hundredth time. He even had me kneel down in the dirt, trying to see where the bullets went."

"He's a thorough man. A man with a lot of experience."

"Has Baker said anything to you about when he wants the inquest?"

"No. Maybe after tonight, when he and the marshal put all the facts together . . ." He stopped as Alice returned. He accepted the drink and waited until the girl left the room. When the door closed, he settled back in his chair and sipped the whiskey. "Frank, there's some information I need from you."

"What?"

He looked at me for quite a while, but I couldn't tell what he was thinking. His face was impassive, and if he was having trouble putting his thoughts together, his trouble was making me nervous.

"What did you need to know?" I prompted again, and he set his glass down and reached inside his coat. He pulled out a single piece of paper.

"This was waiting for me when I got home. I didn't mention it to you then because I wanted you to get some rest, and I felt it was important for White to get the information he needed. And I wanted time to think. Now, we need to talk."

I was getting impatient and reached out for the paper. "Talk about what?" I said as I unfolded it. It wasn't a long message, but I took my time and read it over several times before I refolded it and handed it back. I was furious, but I held my tongue. Nevertheless, I could feel the flush on my face.

"Well?" McCuskar asked.

"Well what?"

The sheriff frowned impatiently. "Let's not play games, Frank. I think I'm entitled to know how someone who spends eight years in the cavalry as an enlisted man can show up in Coffee Creek with thirty-five thousand dollars in cash. I know what the Army pays, Frank, and it doesn't pay that."

A muscle in my jaw twitched, and I met the big man's gaze evenly. "How much do you have in the bank, Doctor?"

"That's not the issue, and you know it," McCuskar snapped.

"What was Rice Patton's reason for blabbing this all over town? I thought banks had rules."

"Patton told me this afternoon when he heard you had ridden out. Yes, it was rumor again, but he didn't know that. He wrote the note to me in good conscience. He told me a bit ago he felt it was information that I might need, as sheriff. Especially with you on the run."

"On the run. Jesus Christ. I was going after a change of clothes. Nothing else."

"We know that now. He didn't know it when he saw you ride out . . . or when he heard that you had. Neither did several other folks."

"You included? You thought I was making a run?"

"I was sincerely hoping you weren't."

"Folks jump to conclusions mighty fast."

"Yes, they do."

I toyed with my glass, and McCuskar leaned forward, expectant. "The money is mine," I said. "It's legal. That's all I need to say." I took a long drink, emptying the glass. "I expect you not to pass that message around any further."

"I'd like to know about the money."

I fell silent and concentrated on rolling a smoke. If that reporter, Jensen, kept his pen alive by plastering my name all over his paper, there was more than an even chance McCuskar would find out about the money, one way or another. Maybe it wasn't such a bad idea that he knew. He sat, patiently waiting, smoking a cigar, watching me through the blue haze.

"It's a long story, Doctor."

"I'd like to know. I've got the time."

And so I told him.

XII

The whole scheme was harebrained from the beginning, but Paul Smith and I were too excited to worry. Three hours into a forty-eight-hour pass from the fort and I was soaking up beer with Smith in an Albuquerque saloon a block off Railroad Avenue. Smith reminded me of my boyhood chum, Stuart Brown, and the friendship between the young policeman and me had been strong since the first day we'd met nearly a year before. That night, Smith was more excited than usual.

"You got yourself a good whore lined up?" I asked him, but he shook his head vehemently.

"I've been hearing bar talk," he said, and he leaned over the table, his eyes bright with excitement. "Guess who's holed up, north of town?"

"President Cleveland?"

Smith grimaced. "Come on, Frank."

"How am I supposed to know? There's a bunch of Indians up there, some wetbacks, probably."

"How about Raúl Sandoval?"

That stopped me short, and I looked at Smith over the rim of my glass. "Says who?"

"That's what I've heard. I've got some spies out there, you know. You have to have, in my business."

"What's he doing up here?" Half the territory was looking

for Sandoval, and that might even have been an underestimation. "Word had it that he went deep into Mexico."

Smith shook his head. "He and three of his buddies are holed up north of town." He grinned, and his voice sank to an even softer whisper. "And I know exactly where."

And that started us. We were too young and inexperienced to be afraid of the scheme we hatched that night over one beer after another. The four men—Raúl Sandoval, Patrick Dugan, Jesús Lucero, and Manuel León—had evaded the law for long enough that they were legend.

Sandoval was the leader, and it was around him that most of the legends grew. I had caught a glimpse of him once, two years before, in eastern Arizona. He'd been running then and was running still. He was no better than any of the lawless that haunted the Southwest then, in rags more often than not, stealing what they could. Sandoval had several killings to his credit, killings of small people who tried to stand up to him. That, and his slippery trail, was what his legend rested on.

What drew attention to the four outlaws this time was the theft of a currency shipment that I contended they never knew was on the train. It hadn't been guarded well and had been unscheduled. When the four hoodlums hit the train, they did so where no one would have expected—out on the flat prairie, where their four fresh horses, in one burst of speed, had no trouble outpacing the locomotive. According to the story from the railroad men, the four took the loot without any suspicions from the engineer or the conductor—not a small feat in itself. When the train reached the Rio Grande, the money was gone . . . more than a quarter million, the rumor had it. Three men on the train were dead. No one, at least no one alive, had seen the deed done. Word of mouth blamed it on Sandoval, and word of mouth said the bandit was headed south as fast as his fleet horse could take him, over two hundred miles of open space, where he and his partners could make time.

There had been a reward for Sandoval for years, the amount varying with the season. But after our talk over beer, neither Smith nor I was interested in reward money. His department and my military superiors were sure to frown on free-lance bounty hunting anyway. They'd frown worse at what we planned that night, but the return outweighed the risks. So we thought.

We did some talking, discreetly, with a railroad representative, and we did some planning. Smith did some more listening, and by the next night we were both so excited we could hardly saddle our horses.

There was no moon, but enough starlight that the big mountain east of the town loomed like a massive shadow in the distance. We lay quietly on the mesa edge and watched the adobe hut below us. If Smith's information was right, the four outlaws were in that hut.

"You think they're in for the night?" Smith asked.

"We'll wait and see. If they're there at all."

"They're there, all right."

"If we know, then others do, too," I whispered.

"We're here first, though." Smith chuckled. "Maybe they think this is the safest place to be, while everybody's hunting south, down at the border."

"Maybe."

"When do you think we should go in?"

"I don't know." I shifted, a little nervous. "I've never done this before. You sure that's the right adobe?" The small hut sat back by itself, close to the thick brush and cottonwoods of the bosque.

"It's the right one. Like I said, I got me spies who owe me." Smith was more confident than I was.

"We'll wait," I said, dubious.

"You think they expect anything?"

"If they're there, no. If they expected trouble, they'd have been gone long ago."

"It's a lot of money. I'd have cleared the territory by now, if it was me."

"Maybe that's why he's been free so long. No one ever accused Sandoval of doing what was expected."

"You really think he didn't know what was on that train?"

"Story has it, he didn't. Just chanced on the right train."

A couple small cactus spines had worked their way through my trousers, and I shifted again, hoping the red ants wouldn't discover me. There was no magic time we were waiting for . . . just time to work up enough nerve to start down toward the bosque.

After a time, I said, "Let's go," and we crept back away from the mesa rim to the horses. I was in civilian clothes, and had exchanged my awkward military revolver holster for one that favored speed. I also carried a .44 Winchester carbine, snout-heavy with eleven cartridges in the magazine. Smith, a three-year veteran of the mud-baked Albuquerque police force, favored a shotgun, cut down and lethal. We rode north along the mesa, then cut down the steep slope toward the river. Our intent was to enter the bosque and approach the cabin from the river side.

The plan worked well. We left the horses in the thickets and worked our way the last hundred yards with our hearts thumping in our throats. When we could see the hut clearly, barely a stone's throw distant, we stopped.

"They don't have a lookout," Smith whispered. I squinted

into the darkness and nodded. "How do you want to do this?" the policeman added.

"Just like we planned," I breathed. There was no wind, and even our whispers seemed like shouts in the quiet night air. We both crouched in that spot for several minutes. There was one light in the hut, filtering out through a single window that faced our way. The doorway was on the opposite side.

I found myself still puzzled at Sandoval as we crept across the smooth sand toward the hut. Maybe he figured he was holed up where gringos wouldn't go—maybe he figured he was untouchable after so long. Whatever the reason, he'd made a big mistake. He'd forgotten that there were amateurs in the world. It was easier approaching the hut than trying to sneak up on any lazy, sleeping hound dog. We reached the mud side of the building without making a sound. There was nothing on the ground to step on, just sand, an occasional cactus, or an ant mound. We made our way around the side of the hut. The ears of Smith's shotgun were back, and my own Winchester was cocked. Smith had said he would go in first, since his scattergun, each load carrying a charge of more than twenty heavy pellets, would do a far better job of coverage than even a dozen rifles.

Around the front corner of the hut we saw the horses tethered off to the south, in the protection of a small copse of cottonwoods. And then came a surprise. The front door of the hut was cracked open, with a stream of yellow lantern light streaming out. I heard Smith's breath catch, but his hesitation lasted only a second. He moved forward quickly, with me at his heels.

We had expected to get the drop on the four men. We expected to parade them, bound and helpless, back to Albuquerque. It didn't work that way. Smith went through the door like a runaway, with me right behind. The four men were sitting at a table, playing cards. Sandoval looked up into the muzzles of Smith's shotgun and my rifle, and his face was as impassive as a rattlesnake's.

"Señors," he said, as if he had been expecting us all along.

"On your feet!" Smith shouted, and I moved to one side, finger tight and nervous on the carbine's trigger. The other three faces turned in slow motion, but I was watching their hands. The four men stood slowly, fingers spread, well away from their guns. "Over against this wall," Smith barked, and jerked his head toward the smooth, bare adobe to his left. We weren't quick enough to make head or tails of what Sandoval did then. Somehow, he sheltered himself behind the others and then made a violent break for the open door. Because Smith had moved away from the men, the outlaw had perhaps eight feet of clear space, and he took the advantage.

The shotgun bellowed, and two men went down in limp heaps, thrown savagely against the wall. A revolver detonated and the slug slapped the wall above my head. Smith dropped the heavy shotgun, and for an instant, while he was clawing for his revolver, he blocked the door from my aim. In that instant, Sandoval and one other man—Patrick Dugan—made it out of the hut. Smith and I tried for the door at the same time, but bullets clipped the mud, and we ended up huddled under cover of the thick walls. The two outlaws weren't waiting for a gun fight. They had the chance and took it, fleeing in the darkness toward their horses. I heard the animals nicker and I dove out the door, firing the carbine in the general direction of the horses, levering round after round as fast as I could while I rolled in the sand. By that time, the two men were mounted, and I levered the carbine again. Smith was crouched in the doorway, holding his revolver tight against the doorjamb, and the flash from the muzzle was nearly blinding in the night. I fired once and saw one of the outlaws lurch. He wheeled his horse toward the bosque, and I fired again, this time at the second man. In the dark, I was sure it was Sandoval. The rifle barked and the man tumbled forward along the horse's neck, clung there for a heartbeat, then fell to the sand. It was over. We could hear the horse of the last outlaw, hit maybe once, crashing off into the thicket. We waited, listening. Other than the barking of a dog somewhere off in the distance, there was no sound.

We didn't need to wonder if the two inside the hut were dead. Smith's shotgun had sent its double charge across the room at head level, and the two men had been tripping over themselves as their leader lunged by, using them for cover. I heard the young policeman's breathing as he crept up to where I lay in the sand.

"You all right?"

"Yes."

"You think he's dead?"

"I don't know. I aim to find out." We approached the dark figure on the ground cautiously, guns cocked. There was no need. One of our bullets, maybe Smith's or maybe mine, had taken the man at the base of the neck. I reached down and turned him over. There wasn't much left of his lower face, but enough. It was Patrick Dugan.

"Sandoval got away."

"I think I hit him."

"Maybe he won't get far, then."

"Maybe."

"I hope to God he didn't have the money with him," Smith said, and his voice shook. He tried for a laugh to cover it up, but it didn't work. My knees were weak, too.

"Let's find out."

We went back to the hut. The place was dense with acrid blue smoke, and one wall was a mess. We both avoided looking at the two bloody corpses on the floor. The money was there, in two bulky canvas bags, each one heavy enough to make a man grunt.

"Holy Christ," Smith murmured when I opened the first one and we looked inside. He looked at me and his eyes were wide.

"We'd better bury those three," I said, pulling the bag shut. "I don't know about you, but I don't want to answer questions from anybody."

"You think the railroad will be good on their word?"

I shrugged. "They'd better be. We could just as easy keep the whole thing, and they'd never be the wiser." I saw the momentary look on Smith's face. "They'd find out sooner or later. I don't want the whole world hounding my tail."

"Yeah," Smith said, nodding. "That ten percent is legal."

"And there's no one who's going to ask questions about these two," I said, looking over at the bodies, "or the one outside, either."

Two hours later, our work made easier by an old, rusted spade we found near the back wall of the hut, we rode back toward the town. The valley was darkly quiet, as if nothing had disturbed the peace that night. The outlaws' horses we had let wander loose, knowing full well someone along the bosque would put the touch to them before the sun set the next day.

The railroad was true to its word. We went to see the top agent just before dawn, and he opened the door for us, wearing his nightgown and holding a small revolver. His eyebrows went up into his tousled hair when he saw the two canvas bags carrying the railroad's brand, and he let us in with alacrity, closing the door quickly behind us. We went into his kitchen and waited patiently while he told his concerned and sleepy wife that she need not worry about the two predawn visitors. And then he counted the money. As he did so, he would glance our way from time to time, the expression on his face skeptical. It took a long time, but neither Paul Smith nor I wearied of watching the bundles of bills pour out of the sacks. When the agent finished, he straightened up, a hand on the small of his back.

"It's all here," he said. "A buck or two short, perhaps." He ran a finger across the neat piles that covered his kitchen table. "Let's say three hundred and fifty thousand. You boys have thirty-five thousand coming, if I figure right."

Smith stroked his lower lip. "How much is there, exactly?"

The agent smiled. "Without counting every bill—I'll have our auditor do that—I'd estimate three hundred forty-nine thousand eight hundred dollars." He tapped one stack. "This one's a bit short." He had better fingers for money than I did, but I was satisfied, and so was Paul Smith. The agent watched us drool, and his smile was faint. "You know, the deal was that your names would never be mentioned. I know Mr. Smith here, but I don't know you." He looked at me, but not curiously. "I can't imagine the Albuquerque Police Department is going to be overly thrilled with your nighttime exploits, Mr. Smith. We're certainly grateful, don't get me wrong. This is a lot of money to lose." He smiled humorlessly. "I just hope you two have thought out your end."

"We'll worry about that," Smith said.

"Then all that's left is to render unto you what you've earned," the man said. "The auditor will no doubt give me trouble about that, too. But then, considering the alternatives . . ." he left the sentence unfinished. We left the man's home with thirty-five thousand dollars in cash and a receipt issued to "persons unknown" that cleared us of the balance. It took the rest of that day before the full impact of what we'd done began to sink in. I think we both did a lot of thinking about leaving the job unfinished. Three men were dead by our hand, but they'd lived with a dead-or-alive bounty on their heads for years. We kept telling ourselves that we had tried to take them in and that they had forced our hand. That wasn't what worried either of us. Raúl Sandoval did. He was out there somewhere, and if he was alive we knew there were two faces he would never forget. And once you knew a face, the rest was easy.

XIII

Sheriff James McCuskar digested the story. He sat quietly, smoking his cigar. His mind was working, and I gave him time to mull over my story. Finally, he frowned and said, "And I'm supposed to believe all that?"

"It's the way it happened."

He tapped a long ash into a brass ashtray. "You're telling me that four professionals let two amateurs walk right in and take them? Where was the other law? If Smith knew, why didn't others?"

I shrugged. "He was lucky."

"Lucky."

"No one ever suspected Sandoval would head north. His stamping ground was the little border towns, where it was easy for him to slip across."

"Then what was he doing up north in the first place?"

"I can't answer that, Sheriff. There's no way to predict where a man like him will move. He did, is all I know. And the law was looking down by the border."

McCuskar laughed shortly and looked sideways at me. "The law. Frank, if someone stole almost a half million, the whole damn territory would be upside-down. There'd be Pinkertons, the Army, U.S. marshals, railroad men . . . you name it. And you two just walked in."

"That's what we did."

McCuskar chuffed out a cloud of smoke and then ground

his cigar stub into nothing. "Then tell me why you have the whole thirty-five thousand, Frank. If what you say is true, you should have half that much. This fellow Smith would have his share."

"Paul Smith is dead."

"Dead?"

"That's right."

"Convenient, I must say."

"Listen, Sheriff," I said, my voice rising, "I really don't give a good goddamn if you believe me or not. I've told you the way it happened. Paul Smith is dead."

McCuskar just gazed at me, hands folded across his belly, no expression on his face. "Maybe you'd better tell me how that happened, too."

"There's not much to tell. We left the agent's house. Smith only had a short time before he was expected on duty. I still had another twenty-four hours on my pass from the fort. We were excited about the money, but we didn't know what to do with it all. We figured to put it in a bank until Smith had time to make his own arrangements. I took the money and did just that. All thirty-five thousand."

"In your name?"

"Yes."

"Smith trusted you, evidently."

"He did." I added, "He had no reason not to." McCuskar raised an eyebrow at that. He had read my meaning clearly enough. "Five hours later, he was dead. Some two-bit drunk put a knife in him."

"And so, conveniently, you ended up with all the money."

"What was I supposed to do?"

"He didn't have any relatives?"

"None that I knew of."

"But you looked hard to make sure."

"No sir, I did not look particularly hard. I never heard Paul talk about family. I assumed he didn't have any."

"Kindly of you."

"Just what are you trying to make me out to be?"

"At the least," McCuskar answered without hesitation, "a young man who doesn't seem to think things through too carefully before he acts."

"I think I did."

"And there wasn't any publicity when the money was returned? The Army never learned of your escapades? Of your vigilante career? Or maybe I should say, your bounty hunter career?"

"The railroad agent said he would keep our names out of it. He kept his word."

"So no one knows—except the railroad and you. And Raúl Sandoval, if he's alive."

"That's right."

"And the Army never questioned your sudden decision to muster out?"

"It happens all the time."

McCuskar took some time to draw another cigar out of his pocket, clip the end with his small penknife, and light it. He looked thoughtfully at the ceiling, through the dense clouds of smoke. "Frank," he said finally, "you are becoming a royal, goddamn pain in the ass, you know that?" I didn't reply. "Is there any chance Sandoval knows who you are?"

"I don't see how he could."

"Is there a chance he would have known Smith? He would have been more visible, I would think, being a city policeman and all."

"Distant chance, maybe. He might have seen him around the city, if he ever took the chance of going there. I don't know. There's always talk. I don't suppose it would have been too hard to figure out who Smith was, if Sandoval asked the right questions. If he asked the right people."

"And if he was able to find out about Smith, he would know about you, wouldn't he?"

"I suppose that could be true."

"That could be true. I'm fascinated by the nonchalant way you allow the world to come down around your ears."

"I did nothing that was illegal."

"Not that that would matter to a man like him. But shooting three men? That's not illegal?"

"There was a dead-or-alive reward for them before Smith and I ever did what we did. And we never put in for that reward."

"How civic-minded. Let me remind you . . . a life warrant on someone means the body is brought back to some law office for verification. An inquest is usually held, or should be. What is not done is to kill and bury and never breathe a word about it. That's simple assassination, and that, my young friend, is not legal . . . anywhere."

"There are people who would argue with you."

"I'm sure." He sighed heavily. "Be that as it may, now you're in another pickle, aren't you?"

"Andy Sorenson's death was an accident, Sheriff. There's no one who could be sorrier about that night than me. But what I did down in New Mexico Territory has nothing to do with what happened here."

"I suppose not. Why you returned to Coffee Creek finally makes some sense to me. It's going to make it a little harder for Raúl Sandoval to find you." He stood up. "Not much harder, but a little. I suppose this village is as good as anywhere for you to hide."

"I'm not hiding."

"Aren't you? Then let's hope Sandoval is dead, because I

don't know too many folks just now that would put them- selves between you and him." He started to move toward the door of the parlor.

"Sheriff McCuskar . . ."

"What?"

"What do you plan on doing?"

"About?"

"Are you going to tell Judge Baker about the money?"

"Would that matter?" McCuskar's gaze was chilly.

"To me it would."

"If things happened the way you say they did, I don't suppose it has any bearing on this case. I'll do some checking . . . discreetly. I just hope . . ."

"Yes?"

McCuskar hesitated. "Forget it." He smiled faintly, just a trace at the corners of his mouth. "By the way, my wife tells me you want to spend the night at the boardinghouse. I'd rather you stayed here until the inquest is over. Probably two more days. By then, we can be reasonably sure. Although why I worry, I don't know. You obviously have a talent for taking care of yourself." He nodded at the door. "Let's go see if there's any dinner left."

XIV

I went to Andy Sorenson's funeral the next day with only terse instructions from McCuskar. He wasn't happy about me attending, but he gave in. "Enter the church when the service starts," he said. "Sit in the back with Judge Baker and Clint White. They both said they'd go. When the service is coming to a close, leave."

That's exactly what I did. The pastor droned on and on, and I didn't listen to much that he said. Instead, I offered a few private prayers of my own, and then just sat quietly, looking either at the polished wood of the pew in front of me or up at the white ceiling. Except for a few turned heads before the service started, I went unnoticed.

Judge Lucius Baker had scheduled the inquest for the next day. He didn't seem to be minding his vacation away from Dalton. White was in and out after the funeral, and I was anxious to hear what he would have to say during the inquest. I spent the day waiting. I would have liked to have spent time with Alice, but she always seemed to have things to do that called her away.

By the hour of the inquest, I was feeling itchy and underfoot—as if I had been penned up. And I had been. McCuskar was adamant, though. I was not to wander about the village— officially or otherwise. It was almost as if he wanted the village to forget my existence until after Baker was finished with me.

The judge had a flair for the theatrical. He held the inquest in the large front parlor of Lulu Grey's boardinghouse. He wanted the public there, and he wasn't disappointed. The room, complete with brocade rug nearly touching the walls and white lace curtains, was far from being a somber court of law. As folks squeezed in and found places to sit, the parlor became stuffy and then smelly with perfume and smoke. The judge had placed a heavy table near the front of the room, directly in front of Lulu's piano. He carefully laid out papers and his gavel and then beckoned at me.

Folks weren't settled yet, and I made my way over to him. "You might enjoy this," he said and smiled. He held out a newspaper clipping. I read it quickly. Wayne Jensen had had a grand old time.

LAWMAN FACES DAY IN COURT

Deputy Shoots Boy, Claims Accident

Buckley Brought Back to Trial by Sheriff and Town Marshal

Frank Buckley, a deputy for Sheriff James McCuskar, was brought back to Coffee Creek to face trial on charges that he shot a 13-year-old boy.

Buckley shot Andrew Sorenson and says the boy was coming out the back window of the village mercantile, a store owned by the boy's father. The deputy sustained a minor wound in the incident.

Although under arrest, Buckley left Coffee Creek for destinations unknown. He was apprehended by Dalton Marshal Clinton White and Sheriff McCuskar, after threatening reporter Wayne Jensen with bodily harm.

I finished the story, ten or fifteen more paragraphs that
rehashed half-truths and guesswork, and handed the paper
back to the judge. He was smiling, but only from the nose
down.

"What's Jensen got against me?"

"Got a way with words, doesn't he?" Baker responded and
pocketed the clipping. He smiled again, this time with some
real humor. When he spoke, he kept his voice down. "Things
come out the way I think they will, you might try some civil
action against him. Course, that might do more harm than
good. Probably best just to forget it. Folks will, in time."

"I'm surprised he isn't here right now."

"He is." Baker inclined his head toward a corner of the
room. Sure enough, the little weasel was sitting in a straight-
backed chair near the door. "Take care what you say," Baker
added, and then dismissed me with a wave of the hand. I
found the chair that had been reserved for me, with Clint
White on my left and McCuskar on my right. I could almost
feel the breath of the people seated behind me. Every chair
in Lulu's house had been put to use, and the windowsills
besides. I wanted nothing more than to roll a cigarette, but
settled instead for sitting quietly, my hands folded in my lap.
Baker cleared his throat loudly, shuffled the papers again,
and rapped once with his gavel.

"Let's get on with this," he said and scanned the sea of
faces. "This is an official inquest called at the request of James
M. McCuskar, sheriff of Dalton County." He paused and
glanced down at the papers, then looked up again. The room
was dead quiet. "Let me remind you all that this is an official
gathering. I will tolerate no interruptions, no displays of emotion, no delays. Those of you who are not called as official
witnesses are here at the indulgence of this court. If any of
you as much as twitches a tongue, I'll have you thrown out.

Do I make myself clear?" He waited a long moment. "Good. I think in cases like this, it's best if there are no rumors, no guesses. That's why I have consented that this inquest be public. It may be unusual, but so is this case." He shuffled papers again and pulled out a long sheet.

"In this case, we're concerned with the shooting death of Andrew T. Sorenson, age thirteen years, two months, a lifelong resident of Coffee Creek and Dalton County. I have in front of me the signed deposition of Sheriff James M. McCuskar, and we'll get to that in due time." He laid the paper down. "Frank Buckley, would you stand, please?" I did so.

"Would you state your age and occupation, please."

"Twenty-eight. Deputy sheriff of Dalton County."

"And how long have you been deputy for Sheriff McCuskar?"

"Five weeks, sir."

"And what did you do before you became a law officer?"

"I was in the Regular Army, sir."

"For how long?"

"Eight years, sir."

"Rank?"

"Sergeant, sir."

"Were you honorably discharged from the Army?"

"I was, sir."

"What made you ask Sheriff McCuskar for this particular job?"

"I didn't ask, sir. He asked me."

"Just so. Are you a native of this area?"

"Yes sir. I was born here."

"Have you been away from this area any time other than your years in service of your country?"

"No sir."

"Would you tell us, in your own words, what happened the night the Sorenson boy was killed?"

I could feel eyes on the back of my head, but I looked straight at Baker and recited what I knew. He listened, eyes half-closed, nodding now and then. There wasn't much to tell. I spoke for maybe a minute, then stopped.

"And you had no idea who was trying to climb out the window?"

"No sir."

"Did you, in fact, know if that person was climbing out, or climbing in, that window?"

"No sir."

"Did you think that perhaps that person was simply sitting on the windowsill, waiting for you?"

"I have no idea, sir. It was dark. All I saw was motion."

"And you fired your revolver only after you felt the bullet strike you?"

"Yes sir."

"How many times did you say you fired?"

"I didn't, sir. I don't remember."

"Hmmm. We'll get back to that. There have been all manner of stories about your actions during the days that followed the shooting." He looked around the courtroom, eyes hard, indicting everyone he saw. Then he looked back at me. "But in the interests of continuity, we'll talk about that somewhat later. You may be seated, Deputy."

Baker called on Marshal White next, and the old man stood, holding his hat in his hand. He was nervous, standing in front of all those people, even though he'd probably stood just that way in a couple hundred trials. He wasn't as nervous as I was.

"Marshal Clinton White, would you state your age and occupation for the record?"

"Uh, sixty-one," White mumbled.

"A little louder, please."

White looked unhappy, but spoke up. "Sixty-one. I'm town marshal of Dalton."

"And how long have you served in that capacity, Marshal White?"

"Seventeen years."

"And you have investigated this matter?"

"Yes."

"Who asked you to do so?"

"You did, sir. And Sheriff McCuskar."

"And would you tell us, in your own words, what you know."

White cleared his throat. He was used to issuing commands in monosyllables, and speeches came hard. "I, ah, looked around some, and talked to some, and I figure it could only have happened one way."

"And how's that?"

"Just the way he says," White said, indicating me. "The boy shot himself tryin' to climb out the window. The sound of the gunshot and knowin' he'd been hit is what made the deputy pull his gun. The angle of the bullets and all."

"Angle of the bullets?"

White groped around for words. "They hit the boy, ah, comin' up, like off the ground. I had the deputy kneel down in the spot, and point his gun. The angle was about right."

"This angle of the bullets thing . . . did you see the body of the boy yourself, or did you just take someone's word for how he was shot?"

"I seen the body."

"Were all the wounds caused by bullets coming from below?"

"No. The wound in his belly was from close up, and angled down."

"It's your opinion, then, that the boy shot himself?"

"Yes sir. First off, he did."

"Would you care to presume how he could manage to do that?"

White shrugged. "Comin' out the window, I guess. It's a right small opening, Judge. No tellin' how he was all scrunched up. Gun went off, and that was that."

"Had you been in the deputy's same situation, what would you have done?"

White hesitated and scratched his head. "I guess the same thing, Judge. The boy's gun went off first. It was dark." He shrugged again.

"One more question, Marshal. What makes you believe the boy's gun went off first?"

White looked confused, and my heart pounded. He didn't answer for long enough that Baker became impatient.

"Marshal?" The question the judge had posed hadn't been asked before, and my palms went wet. When White answered, it wasn't much more than a whisper.

"Don't know," he said. A small ripple of murmurs went through the room, but Baker ignored the noise.

"You may be seated, Marshal. Sheriff McCuskar, let's hear from you." I wiped my palms on my trousers, and hoped the judge wouldn't ask the same question of the sheriff. McCuskar lifted his six feet four inches out of the chair.

"Age and occupation?"

"Forty-one. Sheriff of Dalton County."

"Well, that's half of it." Baker smiled slightly.

"Physician," McCuskar added cryptically.

"Tell us what you know, Jim."

"The boy was killed by either of two wounds. One wound

was through the body, just under the ribs, and caused by a .44 caliber bullet. The other was through the back of the head and caused by a .45 caliber bullet. There was a third wound, but it was inconsequential."

"You have the bullets?"

"I do. The .44 is the same slug that hit Deputy Buckley."

"And the others?"

"They were recovered from the interior wall of the mercantile stockroom. There was a total of four of them."

"Did the boy have a firearm in his possession?"

"We assume so, your honor. One was found, fired once, the next day."

"Where was it found?"

"Inside the stockroom."

"What kind of gun was it?"

"Forty-four Colt, your honor."

"And you think a bullet from that gun killed the boy?"

"I do. There were scorch marks on the boy's shirt. As if the weapon had been fired from just inches away—maybe even actually touching. There was burned cloth in the wound itself."

"And that same bullet hit the deputy?"

"I believe so."

"Is this the bullet?" Baker palmed the distorted bit of lead and held it so McCuskar could see it.

"It is."

"You removed this from the deputy?"

"I did."

"Lucky young man." Baker looked at me and raised an eyebrow. I realized he was a consummate actor. He'd heard all this before, but still managed to look surprised. "Let's suppose some things, Sheriff. Had this bullet not passed through another body first, or some other obstruction, what would have been the result?"

"It would have produced a fatal wound, your honor."

"You're sure of that?"

"Absolutely. It struck Deputy Buckley directly over the heart. Had it not been nearly spent, it would have killed him."

The wound over my breastbone began to itch, but I kept my hands still. "Is there any way, Sheriff, that a wound like that could be inflicted intentionally?"

"I can't imagine any way, your honor."

"I want to ask you a question as a physician, Jim." He paused and chuckled. "Course, I guess I've been doing just that. A man like you who wears two hats, and wears them well, is kind of confusing to us normal folks." There were a couple chuckles in the room, and Baker glared. He turned back to McCuskar. "Did this slug produce a wound that, in your professional opinion as a doctor, was a serious one?"

"It did."

"Was there ever a danger that the deputy might die from his wound?"

"Yes. When I first saw him on the ground, I thought he was dying."

"But he wasn't, obviously. What made you think that he was?"

"He was bleeding heavily. He was scarcely breathing. His heartbeat was irregular."

"So one could say that you were somewhat surprised when you found out that the wound was not, in fact, particularly serious? I mean, the deputy looks fine to me, and it's been only three days, or thereabouts."

"The wound was serious, and the deputy is still far from well, your honor. When he moves about, he usually does so against my orders as a physician. The bullet actually fractured the breastbone, and the force of the blow must have bruised the heart muscle itself. That is serious. He is recovering because he is in exceptionally fine condition."

"I see. There's no way the deputy could have done the damage himself, then, by way of trying to cover up something?"

"Absolutely not."

"Well, then, I have just one more question." My palms went sweaty again. Everyone in that parlor must have been holding their breath in anticipation. "How do you know that the boy's gun, assuming it was in fact in his hands, went off first? How do you know the deputy did not shoot first?"

McCuskar didn't hesitate a fraction of a second. "That would have been improbable, your honor. I have seen the deputy use firearms. In fact, I'm standing here today because of his proficiency. As I said before, the boy had two wounds that were no doubt caused by Deputy Buckley's .45. One was a grazing wound of the arm. The other was a head wound caused by a bullet also at a grazing angle—although it did fracture the skull. We found two other bullets. The deputy's gun was fired five times. Had he not been in the process of collapsing from a serious wound himself, I have no doubt that all five of his bullets would have found their mark."

"But it was dark."

"Even so," McCuskar said evenly. "The distance from where we found the deputy to that window was no more than ten feet. He would not have missed once, let alone the equivalent of four times."

I let out a long, pent-up breath as McCuskar sat down. The judge called several more people—Ben Toby, Ralph Grey, some other townsfolk who had run into the alley after the shooting. Their stories were repetition, but I listened to each one intently. The judge never asked the question about me shooting first again.

"I'd like Carl Sorenson's testimony now," I heard Baker say. I watched Sorenson walk slowly forward, and he stood with head down. His face was impassive.

Baker leaned forward. "Mr. Sorenson, I realize this is hard for you. We'll make it quick, and then you may be excused from this courtroom, if you wish." Sorenson nodded but refused to look at the judge. "Had your son ever entered your store after hours before the night he was killed?"

"I don't know, sir."

"You don't know?"

"I don't know. He works long and hard hours, sometimes, for men like Mr. Toby. Some days, he comes home late. I could not swear that this was the first time."

Baker hesitated. He was leaning forward still, straining to catch Sorenson's soft-spoken words. "Had anything been missing before?" Sorenson shook his head. "Does that mean you don't know, or that nothing was missing?"

Sorenson sighed and his shoulders hunched. "I don't know, sir," he murmured.

"Do you have any notion where your son might have gotten that gun?"

"It belonged to Malcolm Taylor."

"You know that for a fact?" Sorenson nodded. "How did the boy get the gun? Did Taylor give it to him?"

Sorenson was a long time answering, and when he did, Baker had to prompt him to speak up. "I think the boy took the gun from the house after Mr. Taylor died."

"How do you know that, Mr. Sorenson?"

Again the Swede was a long time answering. "I don't see how else it could be."

"What was your son doing in the store that night?"

"I think he was finding some ammunition for that gun," Sorenson whispered.

"He liked guns and such, did he?" Sorenson nodded. "We need an audible answer, Mr. Sorenson."

"He liked guns. He liked any kind of machine. It is as Mr. Toby said, sir."

"Had he asked you for ammunition, would you have given it to him? Would you have given him a gun, if he'd asked?"

"He was too young, your honor." That sentence hung in the air for several seconds before Baker nodded slowly.

"That's all, Mr. Sorenson, thank you."

I watched the man turn and leave the room. He had no stomach to hear any more.

"Sheriff, we need to ask you a couple more things, and then I think we can finish up." McCuskar stood up again and waited for Baker to shuffle papers. "Sheriff, is there any way, any possible way, that Deputy Frank Buckley could have shot the boy, then put that gun from Taylor in the storeroom?"

"No. And he would have had no reason to."

"Then I have one other question, which I normally wouldn't give a hoot whether it was answered in this inquest or not." He leaned forward and clasped his hands together on top of his papers. "Did Deputy Frank Buckley ever attempt to leave your custody after the shooting?" McCuskar looked quizzical. "Let me put it this way. A newspaper in Dalton— THE newspaper in Dalton, has indicated that Deputy Buckley was 'apprehended' by you and Marshal White some distance from town, two days ago. Would you care to explain that for this court?"

"Deputy Buckley was never in custody, your honor. He was under my care as a physician. And he was never apprehended. I heard he had ridden out of town to his own family home to fetch some clothing, so he wouldn't have to wear mine to the funeral. He was set on attending the funeral for the boy, against my medical orders. When I heard he had ridden out, I went after him in my wagon."

"Wagon?"

"Yes. I felt it would be necessary to bring the body back."

"I beg your pardon?"

"Deputy Buckley was not fit to ride a horse the ten miles of that trip—not even one mile. I feared for his health."

"Did you need the wagon?"

"No. I did persuade him to ride back with me, however, trailing his own horse."

"Why did Marshal White accompany you?"

McCuskar hesitated. "He hadn't finished his own investigations of the incident, your honor. I'm not sure he was convinced that the deputy wasn't making a break."

"Was the deputy making a break?"

"No, he was not. He was fetching clothes."

"Was anyone else at the deputy's home, other than White and yourself?"

"Wayne Jensen, the editor of the Dalton *Star*."

"And was there any indication of violence of any kind when you arrived there?"

"No. Jensen was mounted, and his horse was standing several paces from the deputy. Frank was standing, waiting for us."

"Waiting? Was he wearing a gun?"

"He was."

"He made no move to use it?"

"Of course not."

"What did Jensen do? What was his business there?"

"I understood from Deputy Buckley that Jensen wanted information about the shooting of the boy."

"Did the deputy give him any such information?"

"No. Not that I'm aware of."

"What did Marshal White do?"

"He had a discussion with Jensen. The man rode off. We returned to town."

Baker moved his index finger at me, indicating that I should rise. "Deputy Buckley, were you thinking of 'making a break' when you rode out of Coffee Creek two days ago?"

"No, your honor."

"Did you think it made good sense to do what you did? Under the circumstances? Wouldn't it have made more sense to send someone else out after those clothes? Didn't you listen to what Doctor McCuskar had to say concerning your own welfare?"

"I didn't see it that way at the time, your honor."

"Humph," Baker grunted and tapped the pile of papers into a neat stack. "That's all." McCuskar and I sat down. The room was silent, hot and fragrant as we all waited while Baker leafed through his papers, glancing at first one, then another. Finally, he laid the pile down and leaned back. He let his eyes roam the interested faces. When there could have been no doubt that he held all their attention, he said, "I've reviewed the evidence and heard all the statements, as have you all. I've been over to the mercantile myself. I see absolutely no single item of evidence that calls for a trial in this matter. As far as I'm concerned, Deputy Frank Buckley acted properly and entirely within the authority given him by this county and by this state. It is a regrettable incident, an unfortunate incident, but there is nothing to indicate that Deputy Buckley would have fired his revolver, or even drawn it from its holster, if he had not been seriously wounded first—by an unknown assailant, from all appearances." There was a small noise in the corner by the door, and I glanced over. So did Judge Baker.

"Mr. Jensen," Baker said, and his voice cracked like a whip. "You will sit down until this court is dismissed." All eyes turned, and Jensen wilted back into his chair, his hand dropping from the doorknob.

Baker turned back, ignoring the man, and continued his litany as if he had never been interrupted. "We're all filled with remorse, of course, that the young boy was killed, but in this case, there is nothing to indicate that it was anything other than excusable on the deputy's part." He looked at me directly. "I do admonish the deputy to follow orders, however. Deputy Buckley, with feelings running high in town, it was foolish of you to take it upon yourself to leave the village, for any reason, however innocent. You see the kind of talk that results." He paused and swept the faces with a calm glance.

"I would close this inquest with one final remark. It is my considered opinion that Deputy Frank Buckley is serving this community intelligently, diligently, and fairly. Any action he takes in civil court against the libel directed at his good name by the Dalton *Star* is, of course, entirely up to him. If he elects to pursue the matter, he does so with my blessing . . . albeit in some other judge's court." With that remark, Baker rapped the table with the gavel. "Inquest closed."

The first man out the door was Wayne Jensen. One or two people made a point of shaking my hand, but the rest filed quietly out of the room, talking among themselves. I was elated it was over and felt better after Baker's unjudicial remarks about Jensen. No matter what was said, it would gain the man readers, I thought ruefully. McCuskar was busy talking with people, and I slipped out and walked back to the house. I collected my clothes, tying them in a neat bundle. I had about finished when the sheriff walked into the room.

"You're going back out to the ranch?"

"Yes. I think I've imposed on you enough. What do I owe you?"

McCuskar laughed shortly. "The county pays for it, Frank. Not that you aren't capable." He cleared his throat. "What are your plans?"

I shrugged. "You still need a deputy?"

"I still do."

"Well, then . . ."

"I want to see you once a day for a while at least. Make sure there will be no complications."

"All right." I slung the bundle over my shoulder. "Is it all right to talk to Alice?"

McCuskar smiled. "You keep assuming Alice needs her parents' permission to talk to people."

"Well . . ."

"I think she's out back, in the garden."

I walked out of the room with the sincere hope that I would never see it again—not as a patient, anyway. Alice was in calico, pretty as a picture, weeding the squash.

"Hello there."

She stood up and pushed her bonnet back on her head. "How did it go?"

"It went fine. Judge Baker said I did nothing that . . . well, that could've been avoided."

She nodded, then stood on her tiptoes and kissed me lightly on the cheek, then blushed. She brushed her hands and said, "I'm so dirty. But I love the garden."

"I don't mind."

She eyed the bundle. "You're moving back out to your ranch?"

"Yes. It's about time. I feel fine now. I've been underfoot long enough."

"Does Father think that's wise?"

"There goes Father again," I said and laughed. "Yes . . . he thinks it's wise. I was wondering if maybe, later in the week, if you'd like to take a buggy ride, or something, some evening."

She toed a small plant with her small shoe, and then looked up. She tried for a bright smile, but it wasn't working.

"Maybe, later in the week," she replied, and then looked away again.

"What's the matter, Alice?"

"Nothing is the matter," she said quickly, but her eyes said otherwise. "Oh, Frank, it would be so easy to be unfair to you." She looked up at me, and the person standing there was no longer an immature, pretty little girl. Alice McCuskar was growing up. "Frank, sometimes you seem so . . . so . . ."

"So what?"

She shook her head and bit her lower lip. "Frank, I don't want to live waiting for things to happen to me. Did you know that's what you do? I need to make plans. I want to travel. I want to meet new people."

"One place is about the same as another," I said.

She shook her head again and smiled faintly. "No, Frank. I don't believe that's true. Maybe you really think that. I don't."

"Well . . ."

"I just don't want to be unfair to you Frank. I hope . . . I hope you won't think ill of me."

"I could hardly do that," I said, trying to sound more cheerful than I felt. "I'd best be on my way, then. The offer of the buggy ride still stands." I shifted my bundle to the other shoulder. "Don't let those squash get out of bounds."

She smiled, went up on her tiptoes again, and kissed my other cheek. She drew away before I could even lift an arm. The kiss was like a sister might give, and the message was clear. "Take care of yourself, Deputy," she said. I walked toward the livery, feeling a little sorry for myself. It's always rough when you meet up with someone smarter than you are. Maybe what she said was true. I wasn't going much of anywhere fast. Maybe I would have, if I'd stayed in the Army. But that was past. There was thirty-five thousand dollars with my name on it in the Coffee Creek bank, and I didn't have a single plan for it, other than to make sure it stayed mine. That seemed pretty silly. Right then, if Raúl Sandoval had turned the corner and confronted me, I would have trotted him right over to the bank, given him the money, and said to hell with it.

But, as Alice had said so sweetly, there I was, waiting for the sky to fall on me once more. She didn't know about the money. She didn't need to know. She didn't know about Sandoval, either—that I had put a bullet in him, and if he was still alive he would want far more than the money. I had cheated him out of more than a quarter of a million dollars, and only one thing would settle that score.

XV

We had a week of peace and quiet, during which life in Coffee Creek returned to normal. Carl Sorenson still looked haggard and worn on the rare occasions when I saw him in the mercantile. He talked even less than he had before the incident. Ben Toby hired a new man by the name of Bernard Jones, a short, fat, slow-moving fellow who accomplished far less in a week than Andy Sorenson had done in a day. Toby liked to refer to his new partner as "steady," and I guess he was. He never strayed far from the livery. And one thing was sure—any pampering my horse was going to get would be from me. Jones showed only the most perfunctory interest in the animals.

On a Tuesday, I had occasion to ride over to Dalton to deliver another batch of civil papers for McCuskar. The judge wasn't in his office, and I saw no reason to search the village for him, so I slid the papers under his door and left. I was saddle-sore and planned on spending a good hour relaxing over lunch before taking the twenty-mile ride back to Coffee Creek. I had no more than seated myself at the small table in the Wolf's Head when Clint White entered.

"I thought I saw you come in here," he said and sat down. "How's things, sonny?"

I looked at him levelly. "Things are fine." I knew White hadn't come just to chat.

"I thought in your roamin' around you'd do me a favor."

"Name it."

"Keep an eye open for Wayne Jensen."

"What's he done?"

"He ain't done nothing. He just ain't about."

"I don't follow you, Marshal."

"Well, it ain't too complicated. Jensen rode out of town day before yesterday, along about suppertime. He ain't been back since."

"He's free to come and go as he pleases."

White nodded. "I just got a feelin', is all."

"About what?"

"Well," White said, and tipped back in his chair, crossing his arms over his chest, "I saw him ride out. He looked kind of excited, kind of worked up. He didn't have no bedroll with him. I remember that, clear as can be. Remember seein' his coat flappin'."

"So?"

"He ain't the type for sleepin' under the stars."

I shrugged, not particularly interested. "Who knows? Maybe he decided to ride over to Denver . . . or some other place. Maybe he's got a long-lost brother holed up somewhere that he's visiting. Maybe he's got himself a filly somewhere."

White eyed me humorlessly, and his chair thudded forward. "Maybe."

"Something's on your mind, Marshal. Why don't you spit it out?"

White came as close to grinning as he ever did, and he took his time rolling a cigarette. "I just thought you'd be interested, is all."

"The less I see of Jensen, the better. And you know it."

White was holding the cigarette so close to his face that he was almost cross-eyed as he fiddled with the paper. "Maybe.

Maybe so. But I think he's interested in you." I didn't reply and watched White light up. He snapped out the match and tossed it to the floor, then groped in his pocket. "Yesterday, I sort of wondered about old Jensen. His place was unlocked, and I just kind of made my way in. Found this on his desk, layin' in plain sight. Not much, but somethin'." He leaned forward and pitched the piece of yellow paper across to me. There were only three words on it, and a question mark, but they raised the hackles on my neck.

Buckley—New Mexico?

I don't know what White read on my face, but I tried for indifference and said, "You want to tell me what that means?"

"Thought maybe you'd tell me."

"I guess there were lots of other papers on his desk, too?"

"Not on top of this one."

"It's no secret I spent time down in the territory."

"No, it ain't. I just kinda got curious why he was interested, all of a sudden. Inquest is over and done with."

"Couldn't tell you. When, or if, I see Jensen, I'll ask him."

White nodded. "You do that." He stood up abruptly. "I got things to do. See ya." I lifted a finger in small salute as he walked out. The paper still lay in front of me, and I picked it up and thrust it in my pocket.

"You ready for some food now that old grumpy's gone?"

I looked up and saw the Wolf's Head proprietor looking expectant.

"Yeah," I said. "Whatever you've got that's good."

He raised an eyebrow. "All right. Fair enough." A few minutes later, I was tackling the best steak I had ever eaten. As I ate, I wondered how much Jensen knew, and where he was getting his information. If his source was visitors from down south, it was a safe bet that none of us would be talking to Jensen again. I turned my chair so I could see the doorway.

I made it back to Coffee Creek by five that afternoon, walking my horse most of the way. I went to the livery and had Fatso give him a shot of oats, and while my horse was munching, I walked to the McCuskars' as ordered. For once, the doctor wasn't off somewhere, and he saw to me right away, thumping and tapping and humming all the while.

"Looks good," he said, finally. "Wound that almost killed you is healing faster than that damn thumb. It's giving you some trouble, isn't it?"

"Yes," I said. To tell the truth, I had had the urge a couple times just to chop what was left of that thumb off, saving myself some nuisance.

"Well, stop picking at it, and it'll do a whole lot better." He looked at it critically, twisting my left hand this way and that. "Some extra flesh there that really ought to come off."

"I've lost enough of it already."

"Well, I need to trim it up some. That nail root is all whopperjawed. You've got some pressure there that's giving you trouble." He released my hand. "Let's keep an eye on it."

I got up and put on my shirt. "I delivered those papers to the judge." I didn't mention my conversation with the marshal.

"Good. You planning on being around town tonight?"

"Yes. Why?"

"Harriet and I and Rice and Mary Patton are going to ride out to the Flying T this evening." He grinned. "Do a little politicking with Hugh Mullen. He's got the Cattlemen's Association's ear." The Flying T was the largest ranch in the county, and no doubt Mullen held some of the key to the congressional seat McCuskar wanted so badly. "We'll be back late. I'd appreciate it if you'd stay in the village until we get back."

"Of course." He didn't say it, but I knew exactly what was going on in his mind. Alice wasn't going with them, and Harriet would begin to worry as the evening hours dragged on.

And the evening did drag. The town was as quiet as an empty church, even with the moon hanging over the prairie like a giant Oriental lantern. It was so bright there were shadows cast along the street by the storefronts, stairways, even the occasional horse tethered to the hitching posts. Senses become lulled during a time like that, especially if there isn't anything urgent to keep oneself occupied. I circled town, spent some time shuffling papers, circled town again. What Marshal White had to say still nagged, but there was nothing I could do, other than watch, and I tried to do that. I went into the saloon at least three times, nodding to the same four cowpunchers who were playing cards each time I entered. I rode past the McCuskars' enough times that I lost count, still tempted to knock and spend the evening with Alice. Around midnight, I ended up sitting on the front step of the sheriff's office, smoking, waiting. I was so sleepy I could hardly keep my eyes open.

At last, a few minutes before one, I heard the clop of horses' hooves, and McCuskar's wagon appeared at the east end of the street. I got up and mounted my own horse, and rode out to meet them.

"Wonderful night, isn't it?" McCuskar said as he pulled the wagon to a stop. I tipped my hat to the women.

"Any quieter and I couldn't stand it," I said.

"I'd think you'd be ready for some peace and quiet," Patton quipped, and I wondered how long it would be before people let things settle in the past.

"I guess I am," I said and smiled. "I'll be riding out to the ranch."

"See you tomorrow, then," McCuskar said, and I nodded and spurred my horse past them. Out of town, I let the animal settle into his rocking-chair canter and enjoyed the rush of soft, warm air on my face. Somewhere along the way, I decided that Jensen had left the area for good. It must have been Baker's humiliation of him in court that had spurred him. Strange that he had dropped everything, though—all his possessions and all. I covered the five miles to the ranch by the time the moon had reached its zenith overhead. In front of the small barn, I swung down and let the reins hang while I pushed the door open, then led the horse inside to his stall. Enough light filtered through the big door that I had no trouble seeing, and the saddle hit the crosstree with a satisfying thump that marked the end of the day. I put water in the horse's stall, hung the bridle on a peg, and then wiped my hands on my trousers.

"Good night, horse," I said, and turned around to stare into the bright steel of a revolver held inches from my nose.

"Good evening, señor." I had just enough time to realize who was standing there before something came up from below and clouted me on the side of the head.

XVI

Raúl Sandoval sat on the opposite side of the room, half in the shadows, a revolver held negligently in his right hand. Even through eyes still foggy from the rap on my head, I could see he was as calm as the night Paul Smith and I had broken up his poker game. He drew on a cigarette and blew a cloud of blue smoke toward the single lantern he had placed by the dry sink.

"Well, Mister Buckley," he said, and his accent was heavy. "I thought maybe . . . maybe you were going to sleep all night."

I shifted position and found I was tied in the chair with a single rope—not tight, but the knot was behind me. The rope looped around my hands. I would have taken me only a minute to feed it through my hands or to struggle it over my head. In that time, Sandoval could empty his revolver without moving a muscle in my direction. Whatever he was going to do, he wasn't planning on taking long.

Sandoval rose from his chair, uncoiling like a healthy snake. He walked over and stood five or six feet in front of me. "I understand, señor, that you haven't been so well."

"What do you want?"

He stepped forward and reached out with the revolver. He tapped me gently on the head, on the exact spot that was then growing a goose egg. I winced. "Señor," he said, "you are impatient, no? Here I am, concerned about your health. That little newspaper man, he said you were not well."

"Where's Jensen?"

Sandoval grinned, a lopsided smile that was not the least pleasant. "He is a very curious man, señor. A most curious man."

"Is, or was?"

Sandoval chuckled and walked back to his chair. He picked it up and set it closer, then sat down. "You are quick, señor. But let us not worry so much about this man Jensen. We have heard about curiosity and el gato, verdad? He served his purpose, this man Jensen." He gently waved the barrel of the revolver. "We need concern ourselves about him no longer. And you, too, señor. You are curious, no? You wonder, how did he find me after all these months?"

I wasn't about to give him the satisfaction of voicing that curiosity. "What do you want, Sandoval?"

"What do I want, señor? You forget so quick?" He stepped away from the chair and pulled up the tail of his grubby shirt. Not far to the right of his navel, an ugly, deep, star-shaped scar puckered the skin. "You see, señor? You put a bullet in me, no? For some weeks, I was not too well, either." He grinned and tucked his shirt back, using the muzzle of the Colt to push it past his wide belt. "And my three compadres . . ." He shrugged. He hadn't shot me yet, but he was going to, and I started thinking about the rope that bound me to the chair. My hands were in plain sight, and I couldn't do much without him seeing my first twitch. My feet weren't tied, and if he stepped close enough . . .

"It is not so much just to shoot you, señor, that I am here." He walked over to his chair and sat again. His up-and-down pace was enough to keep anyone off balance. He smiled. "That, too, of course." The smile left his face. "And with some

pleasure. But you have something that belongs to me, señor."
I remained silent. Sandoval scratched the end of his thin nose
with the front sight of the Colt. "The money, señor."

"I don't have it."

"Of course you don't, señor. Not here. But somewhere, I'm
sure."

"I don't have any of it."

"Ah, señor," he sighed. "Next you will be telling me that
you spent it, eh? All that money, in so few months? You must
have very rich tastes, no? Señor, you have it, of that I am sure.
And it belongs to me." He shrugged. "It is not as much as I
started with, some months ago. But it is something, no? You
would not be so unwise to say that I have traveled all this way
for nothing, señor. You would not be so unwise as that."

"Why don't you go to hell, Sandoval."

He grinned. "Some day, señor, so shall we all. Some sooner
than others. But for now . . . let me tell you something,
señor. This is a very nice little town you have found yourself.
You know, I stood and watched tonight. I watched you ride
about the village. I watched you sitting on the front step of
that small building that must be your office. Ah, you are
surprised, no?" He chuckled dryly. "It is not so hard not to be
seen, señor. It was so quiet." He gazed past me, as if deep in
revery. "It is a place a man like me would like to settle in,
someday." His eyes snapped back to mine. "But the money.
Maybe you have it in the bank, no? A nice bank, señor. Small,
but sturdy. It would be a shame to tear it down, señor, when I
could simply walk in the door with you by my side. And I
think . . . I think that is what you will do, señor. If that is
where the money is, that is what you will do."

"And if I don't?"

He bit his lip briefly. "So the money is there. Well, señor.
Some men are in more hurry to die than others. If you do not,

I will take that little town apart, board by board." He grinned. "I should find something of value, no? I came for two things, señor." He pointed the Colt at my head. "One is you. The other is the money. I will not leave without the money. And by that time, you will no longer care, one way or another. You and me, señor, we are professionals, no? The others," and he opened his hands, letting the Colt dangle from one finger, "they are small people, señor. Peaceful, simple people. I think they would be very sorry if I have to find the money myself."

I looked at Sandoval's quiet face and knew Rice Patton would never get near his shotgun. The banker may have had the drop on the thugs who had tried to rob his bank weeks earlier, but he wouldn't have a chance to so much as blink when Sandoval charged into the Bank of Coffee Creek. And James McCuskar . . . he would step into it with his mouth doing the talking and Sandoval would cut him down without a shrug. All the rest were merely minor complications.

"Well, señor?"

"We'll get the money."

"Good, señor, good. You are a smart man."

"How do you want to do it?"

"It is so simple, señor. The money is in the bank? These people, they do not know me. We will ride in, when the bank is open in the morning. Then, you will simply take the money from the bank, as is your right, and we will ride out again, no? What could be simpler than that?"

"And then?"

"And then, señor? If you cause me no problems, it is only you, señor, who will die. The people in the town, they will know nothing of it. Perhaps they will find you before the sun, the coyotes."

I have all night, then, you son of a bitch, I thought. *And, by God, I will have you this time.* I sat quietly, waiting.

"We both need a good night's sleep, señor," Sandoval said softly. "It is not so long until dawn." He walked to one side of my chair, and I shifted, trying to keep him in view. He would have to tie me all over again, more securely. Sandoval moved quickly. Before I could turn my head to avoid the blow, the revolver came crashing down again.

XVII

No hangover in the world can produce the ragged awakening suffered after being put out twice by the barrel of a heavy revolver. I became aware of my predicament well before dawn. Not loosely bound this time, I was trussed up like a wild horse awaiting the blacksmith. I lay on my side, feet drawn up behind me, hands tight behind my back. My head banged and my left eye wasn't working like it should. I stifled a groan and turned my head slowly to the side, trying to make out silhouettes of objects in the room. One of the objects was Raúl Sandoval, dozing in my Morris chair like a contented cat.

I cursed him, silently but vehemently, and tried the ropes. Not a fraction of an inch of movement was to be had. After a little more exploring and a little more aching, I lay quietly, the side of my face on the dusty floor.

Sandoval was not a big man, and he was alone. If I could get my hands on him before he shot me, he wouldn't have a chance. I outweighed him by nearly fifty pounds and was at least a half foot taller. There would have to be a time when that revolver of his was not pointing my way. Sometime he would have to swing up on his horse, or wipe his nose, or even twitch an eye. In that time, I resolved, I would be on him, whether my hands were tied or not. And he certainly wouldn't be stupid enough to parade me through the streets of an awakening Coffee Creek with my hands bound—not unless he wanted a war on his hands. But I couldn't let him reach town. Folks there posed no threat to him. He wouldn't hesitate to pull a trigger, but they would. And so I made my decision. The first chance might come when I had to saddle my horse. I didn't see Sandoval offering to do that chore for me.

By the time dawn began to creep into the sod house, I had mulled over my every move. I wasn't much of an actor, but there was a lot at stake. I lay almost on my back, the cool boards hard against my hands. I let the breath rasp a little through my open mouth, and kept my hands closed. Before long, I heard Sandoval move. I kept my eyes closed. He got up, and there were several seconds of silence. I lay like a dead man, resisting the temptation to open my eyes.

The outlaw made himself known by kicking my leg stoutly with the toe of his boot. "Time to stop playing the possum, señor," he said softly, but I refused to move and was rewarded with another kick. I groaned and coughed, and slowly opened my eyes, keeping them unfocused. That wasn't hard. The ever-present Colt revolver stared down at me. Sandoval bent over and pulled a knot near my ankles, and my feet were free. He backed off and motioned with the revolver.

"On your feet, señor."

"My hands," I said, and gasped. The gasp was real. My hands were numb, except for that damn thumb. With the motion of having my legs released, enough blood coursed through it that the throbbing slammed up to my elbow and shoulder.

"You do not need your hands. Get up." He kicked me again, and I cursed. Like a caterpillar, I hunched and came to my knees, every joint protesting. "Very good, señor." He prodded me with the Colt. "To the barn, unless you care to walk to the village, eh?"

I glared up at him in quiet rage. It was his cocky, supreme confidence that angered me more than anything else. "And if I don't?"

He shrugged, as if he couldn't have cared less. "Then you are dead, right now." The hammer of his revolver snicked back. I lunged to my feet, swaying unsteadily. Sandoval chuckled and followed me out the door at a discreet distance. During the short walk to the barn, I tried to work some life into my arms, and the tingle of returning blood brought hope. I stopped at the rough-hewn double doors of the barn and turned to face the outlaw.

"How am I supposed to saddle my horse?"

"Señor, you are a most impatient man," he said, and shook his head. He pushed me to one side and, keeping the gun trained on me, pulled one of the doors open. I saw his horse inside, already saddled. "I hope," he said with a grin, "that you do not think of running, señor. I put you on your honor, no?" He grinned wider and went in the barn. I was never out of his sight as he took the animal's bridle and led him out, keeping the horse between himself and me. "Now," he said, "you can be stupid or smart, no? We will ride into the village like the best of amigos, señor. Your hands will be free." He said that as if he was doing me a monumental favor. "But," and he wagged the Colt as he came around his horse, "you do not have a gun, señor. If . . . if you choose to do something stupid, remember this. I will shoot you where you stand, and then shoot anyone in the village who looks my way. They are your friends, no? If you are stupid, they will be dead friends, like yourself. So you will be smart, verdad?"

I stood still while he reached over with his free hand. The ropes dropped away from my wrists and I rubbed my hands as I turned to face him. The cocked revolver pointed at my gut. He nodded toward the barn. "Get your horse, señor."

I spat on the ground and walked into the barn. I glanced at the pitchfork on the wall, but dismissed the notion. I led my horse out, and took my time with the bridle and blanket. I rubbed the animal's back before settling the blanket. During that time, Sandoval had mounted, and he sat easy with the gun always pointing my way. There was no way to shake his composure, I knew, but his horse might be a different matter. I trudged back into the barn and fetched my saddle. With a grunt, I threw it up on my horse's back. I finished with the cinch and leaned against the horse, looking across at Sandoval. He raised an eyebrow.

"You are waiting for something, señor?"

"I guess not," I said, and grabbed the saddlehorn. I placed the toe of my left boot in the stirrup. Sandoval's horse stood perpendicular to mine, the horse's nose pointed at my own mount's right side. As I mounted, I dug my left toe as hard as I could into my horse's ribs, at the same time yanking the right rein so hard my horse's head cranked around savagely, affording temporary cover as I leaned forward. My weight and the force of the reins forced my horse to dance sideways, turning to the right. Sandoval's horse jerked up his head and spun to the left. It was enough movement to catch the outlaw by surprise and his hand dipped for balance as his horse shied. My horse spun, almost cracking heads with the other animal, and I launched myself away, grabbing for Sandoval's right arm. I was off balance, but I managed a fistful of denim. That was all I managed. I hit the ground. Sandoval's horse finished his dance step and the outlaw was still in the saddle, still with the gun in his hand.

Motion was on my side. Before Sandoval could swing his horse around and bring the gun to bear with any accuracy, I was rolling and diving and running back toward the house. If there was a gun to be had, it would be there. I dove through the front door, hit the floor, and saw my gun belt on the far side of the room, on the small shelf, lying there as neat and welcome as could be. I lunged across the room and yanked the Colt out, then swore. Sandoval had taken his own sweet time in being a bastard. The gun was worse than not loaded. He had taken the cylinder pin out, and the cylinder as well, and no doubt flung them off into the darkness somewhere to rust until doomsday. I dropped the useless gun and turned.

"Señor, señor," Sandoval said. He was standing nonchalantly in the doorway of the house, his own revolver cocked and deadly. I grabbed my useless gun and whipped the piece of metal at him. It thunked into the doorjamb beside his head. He didn't even blink. "And I thought you were smart, señor," he sneered. I dove across the room and crashed to the floor behind the table just as he fired. He was no slouch. The slug from his first shot chewed splinters out of the edge of the table. I upended the table violently, trying to make it to the dry sink. Another slug burned across the top of my right shoulder, but my hand fastened on the wooden handle of a carving knife. I spun around and threw the knife as hard as I could. Sandoval sidestepped and watched, almost casually, as the knife bounced handle first off the wall.

"I never knew a soldier who could throw a knife, señor," he said, but this time he did not smile. He was finished toying with me. "Adios, gringo." I had nowhere to go, but I had a fraction of a second to stare down the barrel of that ugly revolver before Sandoval squeezed the trigger. It takes someone resigned to death to stand still and just let the bullet snuff out life. I didn't have much time, but I tried anyway. I don't know how far I got, because the world fell apart and turned to blackness.

XVIII

For the roaring, crackling, and heat, the only explanation my tortured brain could conceive was a final, irrevocable descent into hell. I opened one eye—the only one that worked —and a puff of hot air blew some of the dust from the floor into my face and into that eye. I cringed, curled up into a fetal position, and brought my hands to my head. My hair was sopping wet and sticky. I jerked one hand away and brought it close to my face. My vision refused to clear, but even so, I could see a bloody mass. If I was bleeding, it had to be a false hell, and I felt a faint relief.

I rolled onto my back. The sky was bright with shooting stars and flames. The stars were sparks, and an ember drifted down and lit on my cheek. It was about then that my brain began to function again. A combination of rolling and crawling brought me to the doorway of the hut, and I choked from the smoke that billowed through the structure. I spent what seemed like an hour with the latch of the door, far above my head. Finally, it opened and I fell outside, rolling in the dirt. My head hurt so that I couldn't think. I didn't care what was happening to my home. All that mattered was to lie still and hope that the pieces of my skull would mend in some fashion before the winter snows came to bury me. Another ember landed on my back, and I made unintelligible noises as I tried to crawl a little further from the house. Ten feet more was a grand accomplishment, and I fell again. My head was turned so that I could look in the direction of my barns. Both were burning, with perfectly symmetrical flames that blew out through two identical sets of barn doors and licked at the two matching piñons that grew beside them. I lay on my side then, watching the flames in fascination. I couldn't remember when I had built that second, matching barn. I rolled my head and stared back at the house. Houses. There were two of them, too.

Everything came back to me then, and I stumbled to my feet. "Sandoval, you bastard!" I screamed and staggered toward the barns. I missed by twenty feet because I chose the wrong one. But there was nothing I could do, other than stand there, hunched over with hands on my head. I could only watch. Once, through the flames, I thought I saw the shape, or shapes, of my horse on the barn floor. By then, the sun was auguring down through my skull, and I turned and stumbled in the direction of a pair of stumpy, matched cottonwoods. I collapsed in their shade, hugged my knees, and rested my head on my arms, cursing softly. Once in a while I would look up and watch the barns and the houses and everything else that I owned go up in sparks.

I had no horse, I had no gun. All I had were the clothes on my back, blurred vision out of one eye that saw two of the world, and a fierce head that refused to let me think of anything but Raúl Sandoval and his calm assassination of my life. But slowly, very slowly, a kind of terrible joy brought some strength back to my limbs. I had my life. I staggered to my feet and left the flames behind me. I made slow progress. Ruts gashed the lane I followed, and they were rarely where my eye told me they should have been. It became like a game played before circus mirrors as I tried to lurch through the knee-high rice grass that grew in the narrow space between the ruts. In the first hundred yards, I must have fallen two dozen times. At each plunge, my head wracked all the more. The more I fell, the more I scraped my hands and knees. My right shoulder burned. I was getting no better at the mirror game, but I was working myself into a hysteria that combined self-pity, loathing, and desire for revenge. Two hundred yards from the burning buildings I heard the first shout.

I stopped and tried to turn, but staggered off to the side of the trail instead, falling heavily. Four horsemen were riding hell-bent from the direction of my ranch.

"Jesus Christ, is that you, Frank?" It was Colin Brown—two Colin Browns, from the spread across the prairie to the east. "We saw the fire. What the hell happened?" His English accent was thickened by the excitement. One of his ranchhands was with him, but I didn't recognize him. Both of him looked nervous. I came to my feet and started to take steps toward them, lost my balance, and went down on one knee. Brown came off his horse in an instant and took my arm.

"I'm all right," I said thickly.

"Like hell. Smitty, bring the canteen."

"Smitty Hays," I mumbled.

"What's that?" Brown asked, and I sat down abruptly. The two Smitty Hayses brought the canteen and handed it— them—to the Colin Browns, who spoke as one. "Who the hell's been all over you? Christ, Smitty, he's been shot to pieces."

"I've got to get to town," I said. I held my eyes tightly closed as Brown pounded on the top of my head.

"Jeez," Hays said.

"What's this, shoulder too?" And I felt hands opening my shirt. "That's an ugly one," Brown said. "We've got to get this man in to the doctor."

"No!" I shouted and tried to get to my feet.

"Easy, son," Brown said. "Easy."

"Horse," I croaked.

"Smitty, I think you'd best ride back and fetch the wagon," Brown said, and Smitty started to turn away. I broke clumsily from Brown's grip and staggered to my feet. By then, I'd had some practice with seeing double, and I collided with the correct Hays. He flinched away from the bloody apparition, and I grabbed his handgun out of its holster. I held it like a club.

"Say now," Brown said, but I interrupted him.

"I need a horse," I mumbled. "I got to have a horse. And I need . . . I need a gun." I waved Hays' six-shooter, and both men stared at me open-mouthed.

"You won't make it fifty feet," Brown snapped. "Frank, have some sense. You've got to have help."

"No." I shook my head, grimaced horribly, and made for Hays' horses. The animal was nervous at the approach of the madman, and it took me some doing to arrange the reins so they'd do some good. I missed the stirrup on the first try, found it again, and swung up, almost continuing on over. I sat on the nervous horse, leaning far forward, my forehead almost resting on the saddlehorn.

"I'll ride in with him," I heard Brown say with some resignation.

"No!" I shouted out, but it came as little more than a squawk. "Sandoval is in town. He'll kill you . . . just let me go." I kicked Hays' horse in the ribs and left the two samaritans standing in the dust, scratching their collective heads. I had a horse. I had a gun. "Sandoval, you son of a bitch," I cried. "You'd better be there!"

I let the horse have his head and concentrated on staying in the saddle. He was a good horse. His lope was easy—so easy any inexperienced dude could have sat the saddle and thought himself a wonderful horseman. I didn't watch the trail. What I would have seen would just have made me dizzier. Instead, I closed my eyes and trusted that animal as I had never trusted any other. The condition I was in, one more fall wouldn't have hurt much anyway. The horse was better at seeing obstacles than I, so I settled at opening my right eye every minute or so to make sure he didn't stray off the road to Coffee Creek.

I had no plan. Raúl Sandoval was not the sort of man to wait patiently for others to negotiate. He would have ridden in and taken the money from the bank—the thirty-five thousand and as much more as he could carry—as quickly as possible. And he wouldn't have stopped to argue with any folks who got in his way. I didn't know how long I had been unconscious in the burning house, but it couldn't have been long. The roof had not yet collapsed when I made it back to life. The sun was still not high. If I was lucky, if they were lucky, someone might have been able to hold Sandoval off long enough. I didn't think then on how little use I was to anyone.

My stolen horse reached the top of the rise just outside of Coffee Creek with me still on board. I pulled him to a stop, gently. Through one bleary eye, I tried to survey the village below me. I couldn't see anyone, but I wouldn't have been able to see a presidential parade if there'd been one. My heart pounded. On the other side of the village, nothing but a green blur, I could see the copse of cottonwoods by the spring, and I turned my horse to the west. I wanted to circle the village and approach from the west, protected by the trees and houses. I would need time, if Sandoval was still there. I was little enough match for him when I was in one piece. I had proved that. As it was, I would be offering him not much more than an easy target. He must have believed he had killed me. He wouldn't make the same mistake twice. And so I had to take my time and think.

I rode west, keeping the housetops in view, and then finally cut south again, walking the horse down the gentle slope. I crossed the main trail out of Coffee Creek and turned again toward the shelter of the cottonwoods. McCuskar's house loomed up, and I rode directly to the back door, my horse taking no notice of Alice's garden when he planted his big hooves. In the shade of the house I pulled up. I slid awkwardly down, my knees shaking. I hung onto the horse. He breathed heavily a couple times and then turned himself into the living statue posture that good working horses adopt when there is nothing to do. I let his reins drop. I was in town and would have to trust my own feet.

Slowly and carefully, I worked my way through the grass and weeds to the back door. I stopped and listened. Nothing. I pulled Hays' revolver out of my belt and squinted at it. My mind was clear, but my eye still wasn't. It was a Colt, and I peered close to find out that it was a .41-caliber—about the most useless thing I could have in my hand, unless I won the opportunity to stick the muzzle down Sandoval's throat before pulling the trigger. Using the butt, I rapped lightly on the door and tried the latch at the same time. It was locked. I rapped again and waited. I rapped again. I felt sicker by the minute. Then my hopes soared.

"Who is it?" the woman's voice asked quietly. It was Harriet McCuskar behind the door.

"Frank," I said. "Let me in." I heard a sharp intake of breath, then some whispers, and then the sound of a bolt drawing back.

"It's open now," I heard Harriet say, but her voice was more distant. Puzzled, I pushed the door open. The revolver was in my right hand, cocked and ready. Harriet McCuskar was standing ten feet inside, an old shotgun in her hands. Behind her was Alice. For a heartbeat, we stared at each other. Then Harriet's eyes flooded with tears. She lowered the shotgun. Alice pushed past her and ran to me.

"Frank," she whimpered, and she hugged me so hard I gasped.

"It's all right, Alice. It's all right." I looked past her, still holding her with one arm. I pushed the revolver in my belt and said to Harriet, "Where are they?"

She had regained some of her steely composure. "Up the street, Frank. There's been shooting, but it's been quiet for the last half hour. James left, and told us to bolt the doors. Ben Toby came running to get him. Ben was hurt. Frank, I don't know what's happening! And look at you! Alice," she said, and stepped forward to disengage her daughter, "fetch some bandages. We've got to do something, before this man collapses in our pantry." She shot the bolt on the door behind me.

"Alice," she ordered again.

I untangled the girl and held her away. "Alice, I'm all right."

"You're not all right," the girl said. Her eyes lost some of the fear. She frowned at my shoulder, and then shook her head. "Every time I see you, you're in more pieces than the last time!" She went back to hugging me again.

"Well put," I said, feeling better.

"Let's see if we can clean you up," Harriet said. She could do nothing about her husband just then, but she could about me.

"There's no time," I said. "It can wait. I'm not as bad as I look." I tried to stand perfectly straight and tall. I was only partially successful. "Does the sheriff have any other guns in the house . . . other than that one?" I pointed at the shotgun, an ancient muzzle-loader.

"I think so," Harriet said, and I followed her through the house. She fetched a Winchester carbine. It was the same one I'd seen jam when I first met James McCuskar in the arroyo.

"Anything else?" I took the Winchester. Harriet shook her head. I levered the light carbine and fed a cartridge into the chamber. I could see another in the tube. "It'll have to do until I find something better." I turned to leave, the dubious carbine in my hands and the worse-than-useless revolver in my belt.

"Frank . . ." Alice started to say. I held up the carbine.

"Later, Alice." I tried to smile. "I will be back, I promise you. And so will your father." I went out of the house to find Raúl Sandoval.

XIX

The closest building to the cottonwoods was Ben Toby's livery. I made for that as fast as my shaky legs could carry me. The big door of the stable was ajar and I lurched inside, breathing hard. The place was empty. I looked out past the door. Up the street, I could see the fuzzy outline of the bank. I shook my head and rubbed my right eye. The double vision was subsiding. By squinting, I could distinguish the front door of the bank. It looked like it might be open. My left eye was swelled tightly shut, and it was difficult to judge distance.

I edged out of the livery. With my rifle held high and cocked, I moved slowly across the space between the livery and the unfinished brick building that stood almost exactly across the street from the bank. A figure appeared in the doorway of the bank. I stopped and held my breath, lifting the carbine toward my shoulder. Even at only fifty feet, I couldn't tell who it was.

"Frank! Get the hell out of the street!" It was McCuskar. I dropped the muzzle of the carbine and dogged across the street toward him. My brain still wasn't working right, because what McCuskar had said, or why he'd said it, hadn't sunk in. Something tugged at my sleeve. At the same time, a gunshot echoed out from up the street. McCuskar ducked back inside, with me at his heels.

"Christ Almighty, you take damn fool chances," the sheriff

said, and then he got a look at my face. "Good God." He took my arm. "Get over here and sit down."

"I'm all right. Where's Sandoval?"

"Up the street . . . in the mercantile. And you sure as hell aren't all right. Christ, I thought you were dead. I thought you had to be, if he knew the money was in the bank. Here, let me take a look at you."

I pulled away from him. I had gotten a glimpse of the interior of the bank, and now I stared. It had been a battlefield. Then I saw a pair of boots over beside Rice Patton's desk. Patton lay on his back. As I looked down at him, I could see only a faint movement of his breathing. A large bandage, stained dark, covered the left side of his chest. I knelt down, but Patton was unconscious. His skin was pasty gray.

"The others?" I looked up at McCuskar. He shook his head.

"They're dead, Frank. And there's nothing I can do for him."

I remained on my knees for a long time, gazing off at nothing, my right fist beating a slow cadence on the floor.

"They never had a chance," McCuskar said. "Ben Toby saw the man ride in. He said the man walked into the bank and then there were three shots."

"And now he's in the mercantile?"

"Yes." McCuskar paused. "Toby got himself a gun from the livery. He had no idea who the man was. When Sandoval came out, Toby tried for him. He thinks he hit him. At any rate, he killed Sandoval's horse."

"And then?"

"Sandoval got off a shot at Toby. Grazed him in the side as his horse was going down. Ben says Sandoval ran up the street, toward a couple horses that were tied in front of the mercantile. Some men came out of the saloon when they heard the shooting. Sandoval killed one of them, then they think he ran out of ammunition. He couldn't very well stand in the middle of the street and reload, and with those guns he didn't have the cover to take one of the horses. He ducked inside the mercantile."

"He's been there ever since?"

McCuskar nodded. "When Toby came to get me and described the man, I knew who it had to be. He was out at your ranch first, then?"

"He was." I got to my feet. "Carl Sorenson's dead, then, too."

"We don't know that. No one can get in there. Anytime someone shows their face, Sandoval shoots. He's got enough ammunition and guns in there to last a lifetime."

"Sorenson's dead," I repeated dully and looked at the sheriff. "He has to be." I looked down at Patton again. "I hope to God he knows I'm sorry this happened. I hope they all know." McCuskar remained silent. "Tell me where the people are, Sheriff, as best you know."

McCuskar walked over toward one of the windows, keeping out of the direct light. "Ben is over in the saloon, along with at least five others. There are a few men on the other side of the mercantile, in the boardinghouse." He turned away from the window. "There's even one man with the pastor at the church. Sandoval is covered, Frank. There's nowhere he can go."

I looked out the window. The horses were still there. To me, they looked like big shadows standing in front of the store. "Unless he makes a break and gets one of the horses."

"He'd be cut to ribbons before he had one foot in the stirrup."

"Sieges don't work when the man on the inside has all the food and all the weapons, Sheriff. Sandoval can live in that mercantile for years, if he has to. The only way you're going to get him out of there is either to rush him or burn the place down. He sleeps like a cat. He'd hear you approaching anytime."

"Either way," McCuskar said, "you kill folks who have no part in this. We'll wait."

"Wait? For what? He's not going to just walk out of there and let us shoot him."

"I don't know what we'll wait for, Frank," the sheriff said angrily. "Damn it." He smacked the wall a resounding wallop with the heel of his hand and turned on me. "Damn it, Frank, I do . . . not . . . know what to do! I'm not the goddamn cavalry! I'm not ready to just charge in and wipe the slate clean of men like this Sandoval." He glared at me. "And neither are you. But I'll tell you one thing, young fellow. I am not about to see another single one of these innocent people shot down. Sandoval can sit in that mercantile until it rots down around his ears. If it means a chance for whoever might be in there with him, we'll wait forever." He jerked his head toward where Patton lay. "These people are friends of mine, Frank." He wiped his face with a big hand. "Christ," he breathed, shaking his head slowly. "When did he find you?"

"Last night—he was in town all along."

"What happened?" McCuskar looked at my head and frowned.

"I tried to jump him. He came last night, got the drop on me. I should have taken his deal."

"Deal?"

"He offered to ride into town with me, get the money, and leave."

"And you jumped him."

"I tried."

"I see." McCuskar reached over and turned my head and

peered closely at the wound. "Must have been a hell of a fight."

"No. I had no gun. He must have thought I was dead after he shot me in the head. Then he burned the place."

"You're a sight. Let's see what we can do."

"It can wait, Sheriff. It's time folks stopped worrying about how I feel and think some on Sandoval."

"You're in no condition to do anything. You can't even see straight."

"I can see just fine."

"Like hell," McCuskar grunted. "You feel your way around like a blind man, Frank. For God's sake, look at yourself." He grabbed my left arm and led me across the room to the Thomas clock. A gold filigree mirror covered the pendulum case, and I stared incredulously at the apparition that looked back at me. My left eye was swollen shut, and Sandoval's bullet had dug a gutter in my scalp from the corner of my left eye back to my ear. It had bled profusely, soaking the left side of my head, caking in my hair, and drying on the side of my face—a thick brown mess from nearly the top of my head to my shirt collar. I leaned forward and put a finger to my eye, and McCuskar caught my hand.

"Leave it be, Frank." He put his own fingers expertly on my scalp. "That's quite an egg, too."

"He hit me twice. With his gun, by way of persuasion."

"And the shoulder?"

I looked down. The right side of my shirt was brown, too. "His first shot."

"A man can only take so much abuse, Frank. We'll wait out Sandoval. It may take from now until Christmas, but no one else is going to get hurt. And that includes you."

"No."

"I mean what I say, Deputy."

"Then take me off the payroll." I started to fumble at the badge on my shirt.

"Don't be an ass, Frank."

"Then unless you're willing to hit me again, stay out of my way." I returned his glare with one bleary eye. "And I mean that."

"There's nothing you can do. Nothing. He's got a clear sweep of the street from the windows over there. He can stand back from the glass and we never see him. The sun's wrong. There are no windows on the sides of the building, and only the one in the back. That's too small to do us any good. A man couldn't climb through without being heard, and no one could protect himself while he tried. I've got two men in the alley behind, watching. Just in case Sandoval tries. There's no other way for you to get in there."

"I'll find a way."

"And what about the others . . . the others in the mercantile. You've thought about them?"

"Sorenson?"

"Him. We don't know who else might have been in there. Could be almost anyone, middle of the morning like this."

"Sorenson's dead," I repeated. "So is anyone else that was in there."

"You don't know that."

"I know Sandoval. If he'd wanted a hostage so he could make a break, he'd have done it long before this. No, he got the drop on Sorenson. It wouldn't have been hard for him. I'm sure as I can be that the only man alive in that mercantile is Raúl Sandoval. You say Toby's over at the saloon?"

"Yes. What do you plan to do?"

"I want to talk to him. He helped Sorenson build that store. Maybe he can be of help."

"You can't get across the street without Sandoval seeing you. You'd be in plain sight."

"Then you keep him busy," I said. "He missed me when I walked over here. Maybe we'll be lucky. Maybe he'll miss again." I handed the carbine to McCuskar. "Use this thing, if it'll shoot," I said. "I want your revolver." I held out my hand. He hesitated, then pulled the gun from his belt. It was a .45. I tossed Smitty Hays' .41 to the floor. "Smitty Hays lent me that and his horse. I saw him and Colin Brown on the trail near my place. I hope they don't come riding into the middle of this." I checked the loads in McCuskar's revolver and snapped the gate shut. "Keep him busy, Sheriff."

"The other side of the street is that way, Frank," McCuskar said, but he wasn't smiling.

"I'm not that blind."

"Let's hope not."

I moved to the door. McCuskar stood in the middle of the bank's floor, carbine in hand. "You going to cover me or not?"

He nodded and went to the window. The glass was already shattered. I took ten seconds to draw a couple deep breaths, then lunged out the door. The crash of the .44 carbine was loud in my ears, and as I raced across the street the cadence of the shots came regularly—five, six, seven, eight of them and I was beyond Sandoval's range and into the saloon. I stopped just inside the door and bent down with my hands on my knees.

"Good God," someone said quietly, but I didn't look up. I was too busy trying not to pass out.

"Where's Ben?" I finally gasped and straightened up. Two men were near the window of the saloon. Ralph Grey was in the back with two other men.

"He's back here," Grey called. I made my way through the

tables. Toby was sitting in a straight chair, face chalky. He was holding a pad of gingham cloth against his side.

"You all right?"

Toby nodded. "Just hurts like hell. McCuskar says it didn't get past the ribs. You ain't so hot-lookin' yourself."

I drew up another chair and sat. "Ben, you helped build that store, didn't you?"

"Yup."

"What's up above?"

"What do you mean?"

"Between the roof and the ceiling. There's got to be space there."

"Yup. About enough for the birds and squirrels to make a mess. Full of trusses. A kid couldn't crawl his way through. And except for twelve-by-twelve vents, there ain't no way to get up in there, neither."

"Shit."

"Yup."

Grey frowned. "Say, who is this guy, anyways, Frank?"

"He's a bad 'un, I'll vouch for that," Toby said fervently.

"He is that," I said. "His name's Raúl Sandoval. Used to head a gang down in New Mexico Territory." I took a deep breath. "Lawman friend of mine and me killed three of his partners, got back a currency shipment they'd stolen. Railroad gave us ten percent. Only mistake we made was not being able to kill Sandoval, too. My partner got killed. I had the money. Took Sandoval this long to find me. My mistake to figure he never would. I put a bullet in him when we took the money. He figured to even the score—and leave with the money."

Grey snorted. "Looks like he's made fair progress makin' it up to you, Frank. He ain't got the money, though. What he took from the bank still lies in the street, up there with his horse. Ben shot it right out from under him."

Toby was watching my face. "What you aim to do?"

"I don't know. I thought maybe I'd be able to get through the ceiling somehow."

Toby shook his head. "Ain't possible, Frank." He straightened in his chair and winced. "You know, young fella, there ain't nothing you ever did when you was a squirt that matches what you brought to this town now." Toby was the first one to remind me of that, and it went down hard. I turned on my heel and walked to the front door. I hadn't seen him when I ran across the street, but I could see Sutton Reynolds now. The cowboy, one of the saloon's habituals, was lying in the street near the boardwalk, his head twisted toward me. There was a bullet hole in his forehead.

"Where you going?" Grey called after me. I ignored him and left the saloon. Staying close to the wall, I worked my way along the front of the saloon toward the mercantile, revolver ready. Safe beside the towering sides of the store, I walked quickly around to the rear. I saw a man standing some distance away, sheltered by an outbuilding. I ignored him and crossed to the small, shuttered window. The shutter was latched from the inside. I put my head as close to the wall as I could and put a finger under the edge of the shutter. By pulling out gently, I could see the glint of the metal latch. There was enough space there for a slender knife blade. I stepped quietly away from the wall and went back to the saloon.

I outlined my plan to the men there. Ralph Grey wasn't happy. "It won't work," he kept saying.

"I can get across the street," one of the men who had been waiting at the front of the saloon said. He was one of Hugh Mullen's men from the Flying T. He was nervous, but game.

"Make sure McCuskar understands," I said. When we went out the saloon door, I worked my way over to the front corner of the mercantile again. Another step toward the street and I would be in front of the building, exposed to the windows. I looked back. The cowpuncher, agile and in far better shape than I, was crouched in the door of the saloon. I had two revolvers—McCuskar's .45 and Ben Toby's. I sidled as close to the windows of the mercantile as I dared, both guns held high. I glanced back at the cowpuncher and nodded. Without waiting, I snapped my right arm around and fired through the glass into the store, thumbing the revolver as fast as I could, swinging the barrel to splatter the bullets across the interior of the store. The gun clicked empty and I dodged back for cover. I caught a glimpse of the cowpuncher diving through the doorway of the bank.

"Sandoval!" I shouted, and then had a moment of panic when I realized he could as easily shoot through the walls of the store as not, and the sound of my voice had given him a vague target. I changed position, moving forward toward the front corner of the building. The corner of any frame building I had ever seen was a mass of solid studs, and there was no gun he would have that could penetrate an inch of interior wall, then six or eight inches of wall studs, and finally the outside boards. I hoped there wasn't. The rest of the building might as well have been paper. The corners were safe.

"Sandoval!" I shouted again. "I want to talk to you!"

Again, there was silence. "Sandoval, you yellow-spined son of a bitch! I want to talk!"

"About what, señor?" His voice was so close I involuntarily jumped. I contemplated shooting through the wall, and he was probably thinking the same thing. But our voices were muffled and distorted, and we'd both be wasting ammunition. As it was, we had to raise our voices to be heard. "You are a very hard man to kill, señor."

"Give it up, Sandoval. You're not going to get out of there."

"We will see, señor."

"Make it easier on yourself, Sandoval. Walk out of there with your hands up." He didn't bother to reply to that. "In about two minutes, we're going to punch this building so full of holes from every direction that a mouse won't be left alive."

There was a faint chuckle. "Señor, wouldn't it be less expensive for you just to burn it down? I don't think your head is working too good. And what about the storekeeper? You will do this with him in here, too?"

"He's dead and you know it."

"You are perhaps thinking better, señor," Sandoval said, and he laughed again.

I was stalling for time and watching the back corner of the mercantile. Nothing yet. "I'm going to come through that door, Sandoval. You've killed innocent people for no cause. You're nothing but a butcher."

"It is interesting you say that, señor. You were given an opportunity earlier and chose not to take it. If you are impatient, señor, then I suggest you do what you say. Come through that door, señor." He kept talking, but I was already moving. Seeing my motion from across the street, gunfire erupted from the bank and the church. Behind the saloon were Ralph Grey and the second cowboy from the saloon. They had upended a rain barrel under the window, which now hung open. the cowboy held a carving knife, but he wasn't grinning with his success. He was too scared. Without hesitation, I scrambled up on the barrel. I was able to look into the stockroom of the mercantile.

The door from the stockroom into the store proper was

closed, and it was tight enough against the jamb that I knew it was still fastened securely. Locked or not, it would put me closer. Keeping Toby's gun in front of me, I slipped that arm through the opening and forced my shoulders obliquely through. It was a narrow fit. I left some skin behind. I lay still for a moment, catching my breath, the sill hard against my belly, my heart pounding with anticipation of what was to come. I cocked the revolver, keeping it pointed at the doorway to the interior of the mercantile. McCuskar and his friends across the street were doing their job well. From the bank and from the church came the methodical slamming of gunfire. With those shots came the shattering of glass as the front windows of the mercantile, what was left of them, exploded inward from the hail of fire.

I stiffened my legs and a second later felt the violent shove on my boots. I pushed with my arms as well. I went through the window like a cork from a champagne bottle, skin scraping off my legs and shins. I twisted as I was pushed, trying to keep my legs bending the right way. I fell heavily down the interior wall of the stockroom, trying to roll and keep the revolver in the clear. Even so, I landed in an ungainly heap, but the revolver was trained on the doorway. I lay still, breathing hard, head pounding. The shooting from across the street had slowed but still thudded out. Sandoval hadn't wasted a shot. His gun was silent. Where he was in the store was anyone's guess. I got painfully to my feet and ducked behind a pile of boxes and reels of barbed wire. With that as cover, I made my way to a point near the stockroom door. With one finger, I pushed gently. The door, built to open into the store, was bolted.

I wanted nothing more than to burst through that door, gun blazing. I forced myself to stand still and think. The door was secured by a single sliding bolt. It would take a solid blow to bust it out of the jamb. Beyond the doorway was a narrow aisle that passed between the counters. And beyond that was the welter of stock that was the character of the mercantile—cracker barrels, wood stoves, displays of bolted cloth, hardware of every description, hanging lanterns—anything the mind could imagine. Somewhere in all that mess was crouched Raúl Sandoval, waiting like a patient cat, confident and invulnerable. If the shooting by McCuskar and the others had done its job, Sandoval had heard nothing of my entry. If it hadn't worked, the outlaw was grinning with pleasure, his gun trained on the stockroom door.

XX

A second flurry of gunfire bellowed out from across the street. With a dull *pock* one slug came through the wall of the stockroom, high up by the ceiling. I ignored it. McCuskar had then crossed the street, if he had followed my directions, and he would be working his way to the front corner of the mercantile. I hoped the cowpuncher had told him exactly where to stand to protect his considerable bulk from Sandoval's bullets.

McCuskar must have cursed my plan, for I had forced him into it by proceeding on the assumption that he would do his part. That left him little choice, and he wouldn't like that. He was no coward, but gunplay wasn't his profession. I was in no mood to extend Sandoval's life a moment longer than necessary, risk or no. I set the position of the counters beyond the door firmly in mind and checked my revolver. If the outlaw was crouched behind the counter, I would have little time— no time—even to focus one bad eye.

I backed up five steps from the doorway, checked my revolver once more, took a deep breath, and plunged forward, driving all my weight and all my strength against the stockroom door. My left shoulder hit it right where the bolt passed into the doorjamb. It shattered inward violently, swinging all the way around to crack into the wall. Before wood contacted wood, I snapped a shot into the space behind the counter. I was off balance, and the slug dug into the wood floor long before my brain registered that Sandoval was not there. With no attempt to search out his hiding place, I dove to the floor. He was fast. Across the store a gunshot exploded. The glass display case above my head shattered. Glass fragments pelted down. Simultaneously McCuskar's gun boomed from the front corner and I heard Sandoval curse.

"Stay out of here, Sheriff!" I yelled as loud as I could. I lay still, my revolver in front of me. Above, inviting, stood a row of shotguns and rifles. A chain held them secure, and the chain was locked with a padlock.

"You are very good, señor." Sandoval's voice floated across from the other side of the store. He had chosen a fortress of linen bolts for protection.

Keep talking, you son of a bitch, I thought and squirmed my way along the length of the counter. Up in the smashed display case were the handguns. I gently reached up and ran my hand along the shelf until I felt metal and wood. I grabbed the gun and brought it down. It was a new .44. The cigar box of assorted ammunition was still under the counter. As quietly as I could, I gathered six rounds and loaded the revolver. Sandoval wasn't moving. I took time to sort out seven .45s. One I put in Toby's gun to replace the spent round. The others I dropped into my shirt pocket. With a revolver in each hand, I pulled myself along the length of the area behind the counter.

"You are very persistent, señor. And you must be in pain, verdad?"

You're worried about that, I thought. *And you keep talking.* Protected by the cracker barrel, I slowly moved my head so I could peer around the end of the lower section of the counter. I could see the tops of the linen bolts. They rested on a series of planks that in turn topped a row of wooden barrels. I could see the barrel at the end of the row. On top of it and the plank rested one of the new-model stitching machines. By turning my head, I could see partially down the center aisle of the store.

Carl Sorenson lay in that aisle. Between his shoulder blades, driven in to the hilt, was a knife. At the sight of that gentle man lying there the bile rose in my throat. I gathered my legs under me and lunged across the open space between the counters, firing both guns as I did so. If Sandoval hadn't moved, the six feet of counter and then two feet of empty space separated us. Once around the end of the counter, I would be able to see directly down the wall, with a clear field of fire. The linen bolts would protect him no longer.

From his position, the outlaw could also cover the front of the store. There was no way for McCuskar to make a move— even if he knew how—without exposing himself to murderous fire. I had both guns cocked when I heard commotion from the stockroom. There was a loud thud and a clatter, and I knew someone else had come through the window. I swore. He'd walk into the middle of this, and whoever it was, probably the eager, scared, and inexperienced cowpuncher, would end up shot full of holes. I heard a scraping from Sandoval's position and gave up waiting. I threw myself down the length of the counter, hitting the floor on my right shoulder, both guns firing wildly into the space where the outlaw should have been. He wasn't. There was a crash from the center of the store, and a gunshot from the stockroom. Sandoval's gun exploded, and I heard a yelp from the rear of the store.

I was on my feet and firing. As the outlaw ducked behind a display of galvanized buckets and black coal scuttles, I saw one of my slugs take him in the left elbow. From the way it hit, I knew it had gone through the arm and then into his side. He slashed at the buckets with the barrel of his gun, and fired in my direction.

The cowpuncher ducked through the stockroom doorway and fired once, wildly, before landing behind the protection of the counter. In that second that my attention was diverted Sandoval snapped another shot at me, and a giant club drove me backward until I hit the wall. I struggled to keep my balance, concentrating only on lifting the heavy guns. Even though he was then standing in the clear, with no protection, the outlaw made no move toward either me or the cowpuncher. Out of the corner of my eye I saw McCuskar in the doorway, crouched low. Sandoval turned slowly on his heels, his face slack, the revolver in his hand sinking until his arm hung straight down. The roaring of my burning ranch was loud in my ears. My guns finally came up, and Sandoval was flung like a rag doll across the aisle as my guns and McCuskar's roared simultaneously. I didn't see the outlaw hit the floor. I had had just time to squeeze the two triggers before my knees gave out. I slid slowly down the wall and sat with my back against the boards. I let my head fall back and I rested. I felt heavy, and numb, and tired.

"You had to do it, didn't you?" McCuskar's voice floated through the fog in my head, and I opened my one good eye. He was standing over me, the revolver still in his hand. He tossed it to one side and knelt down. "You're a goddamn fool, Frank."

"I didn't want any more mistakes," I said. His hands probed. I promptly fainted.

XXI

Sandoval came close to having the last laugh. For the better part of two weeks, James McCuskar and his two nurses sweated at keeping me alive. A little chunk of something left behind in the wound made life a hell for all of us. I hemorrhaged, fevered, and went delirious.

By the time I could stand beside my bed without assistance —it certainly was my bed by that time—it was the better part of August. The village of Coffee Creek had healed slowly, too. Someone from up north came and took over the bank. Rice Patton's widow took her two children and went back east somewhere, to forget that Dalton County existed. Carl Sorenson's widow elected to run the mercantile herself. It was all she had left, and she remained there to make the best of it, a dour and unhappy woman. Ben Toby healed up, and at one point over a beer he asked McCuskar if I "had any more friends" that might show up. The doctor never told me what he replied to the liveryman.

From my window, I watched the town come back to life, and wondered more than once what my part in it would be. Occasionally I tried to talk to McCuskar, but he always waved the subject off, saying something like, "We'll talk about it when you're on your feet, Frank."

I was on my feet, but I didn't know where I stood. One morning, I was in the parlor, watching a squirrel launch himself from one limb to another in search of something.

Maybe he was just having a good time. Alice McCuskar entered, and I returned her greeting without turning from the window.

"What do they think out there?" I asked.

"Who?"

"Folks in town. What do they think? What have they been saying?"

"I don't know." She didn't sound convincing.

"Yes, you do."

There was silence, and I turned away from the window. She was dressed in calico, her gardening dress. "They wonder where you'll go," she said quietly. "If you'll go. What you'll do."

"Do they want me to go?"

"I don't think so. My father was telling us a few nights ago that Colin Brown was in the saloon, telling for the hundredth time how he and Smitty Hays found you staggering down the road to town." She smiled faintly.

I grunted. "There wasn't much of anywhere else to go, Alice."

"You could have gone the other way."

"Now you're trying to make me out a hero. There were some good men killed because of me."

"And some good men saved, Frank. I don't think you give people enough credit. They remember the good, too. Things balance out."

I turned back and watched the squirrel disappear into a big rotted hole in the cottonwood. "Your folks still planning on going back east? To Washington?"

"Yes. Father says we're going. Whether he wins the election or not."

"He'll win it."

"We all hope so." She hesitated for just a fraction, then said, "You should run for sheriff."

I turned and grinned. "You are a dreamer, young lady."

"Father says you could win, if you took it one step at a time, and planned ahead. It's a year and a half away."

"Father says," I mimicked, and we both laughed.

"Well, he does."

"He never said that to me."

"He's been busy trying to keep you alive. And politicking . . . on his own behalf . . . and yours."

"And what do you think, Alice?"

She clasped her hands in front of her. "This is your home. Coffee Creek and Dalton County is where you were born and raised. I think people in town are waiting to see if you are just a drifter, or if you're home to stay." She smiled and touched me on the shoulder. "I think it's time you admitted to yourself that this is where your roots are, too."

"I did that on the way into town."

She nodded. "You're good at your job, Frank."

"If I was good at doing anything else, maybe I would be tempted to give you an argument about that," I said. "But I'm not, except I was learning to dance, a while ago." She smiled, and it looked encouraging. "You think that maybe, in the next year and a half, there'll be a dance you might like to attend?"

"I think most likely, Frank."

"The dancing sheriff. I could build an interesting reputation on that. But right now, I have other things I need to worry about."

"Like?"

"Like finding two nickels to rub together, so maybe I can buy a horse from Ben Toby."

Alice's face turned serious, and I laughed. "Next you're going to tell me your father says I shouldn't ride yet."

"No, I wasn't going to say that . . . although you shouldn't. I was wondering . . . when you mentioned money."

"Yes?"

"I was wondering why you gave the thirty-five thousand to the county and not . . ."

"To the widow ladies?"

"Yes."

"I tried, by way of your father. He's better at diplomacy than I. He said they refused." I shrugged. "I didn't want it anymore."

"No one knows that."

"Except your father and me. And the two women. And now, you. No one else needs to know."

She smiled. "The same old Frank. How many more secrets have you hidden, tucked away somewhere?"

I held a finger to my lips. "If I answered that, they wouldn't be secrets, would they? But," I added, "I think I'm fresh out. Unless you want to help me steal your father's wagon this afternoon. We can ride out to the ranch and pick a spot for me to build another house."

Alice beamed, then frowned with mock seriousness. "I don't think Father would think highly of that."

"He doesn't have to know, does he?"

Alice McCuskar laughed happily. "No, Frank. He doesn't need to know." She shook her head in exasperation. "You know, when I'm in Washington . . . you're going to seem very far away. I'm going to miss you."

"I hope so." I ran a finger down her cheek. "Why don't you get your bonnet? I'll have Ben hitch up the horses."

P011 "You really think you should?"

About the Author

Steven Havill has worked as a reporter, a photographer, and an editor in New York and in New Mexico, where he now lives. He is the author of two previous Double D Westerns, *The Killer* (1981) and *The Worst Enemy* (1984).